This book was donated by
Katie Flowers in memory
of Bob Flowers.
WITHDRAWN
© DEMCO, INC.—Archive Safe

OUTLAW'S JUSTICE

A.J. Arnold

FAWCETT GOLD MEDAL • NEW YORK

A Fawcett Gold Medal Book
Published by Ballantine Books
 Published in the United States by Ballantine Books, a division of Random House, Inc., New York, and simultaneously in Canada by Random House of Canada Limited, Toronto.

Library of Congress Catalog Card Number: 92-90607

ISBN 0-449-14805-X

Manufactured in the United States of America

First Edition: October 1992

To Dave "Quick Draw" McGraw, friend and expert on historical guns and their ranges.

Chapter One

****

Only three players were left in the game when the down-at-the-heels cowboy threw in his hand.

"I'm out. You've cleaned me. There's just enough left of my poke for one shot of rotgut. Think I'll ride the grub line north. I hear there's plenty of open range and new outfits up in Montana. That ought to mean I could get a job riding."

He pushed his chair back and went to the bar, where he was served by a tired, bored man.

At the table the gambler riffled the deck. "You said your name is Clay?" he asked the other player.

The blond young man glanced up quickly. Somehow the gambler's face looked different now, so he responded in a friendly tone.

"Yes, Clay's short for Clayton. It's all I've used for several years now."

The gambler stopped just short of a smile. "One name is plenty out here on the plains. However, this town knows me as Merle Hollister. Other times and places, other names."

Clayton didn't answer. He waited, wondering where the conversation might be headed.

"How about some advice from a man who's a bit older and a lot more experienced?" Hollister suggested, his voice low and deep. "Don't play cards with a professional like me."

The gambler dealt them each a hand. When he finished he

said, "Play this like you had some money. Not a lot, but enough to bet."

Clayton studied the man's creased face and near-black, dead-looking eyes. After a moment he thought, why not? and glanced at his cards.

He said, "I'll open. Five dollars." After all, it was only make-believe, and he had a good start on a flush.

The hand went on. Each man bet more and more. Clayton finally got the card he needed to finish his flush and stood pat.

"Call," Hollister said.

Clayton showed his flush; then the gambler turned over his hand. Clay was looking at four of a kind.

Hollister pushed his flat black hat farther back on his head. "See how easy it is for a man who knows how? I didn't cheat in the game tonight. I didn't need to. But I did with this hand, and you didn't even see the difference."

Clayton felt the angry red crawling up his neck and onto his thin, angular face. Then he thought, well, what the hell? He never *had* been any good at poker.

He asked the gambler, "Why'd you show me that?"

Hollister was so long forming an answer that Clayton figured he wasn't going to say anything. But when he did, it was in that quiet, deep voice as if to make sure nobody else could hear.

"I watched you play tonight. The others were all more experienced, and they all came out of the game with less than they started. You're the only one who even came close to breaking even."

Clayton looked at the neat, hard little man, noted his black-vested suit, expensive white shirt, and black string tie made into a natty bow.

"I don't understand," Clay said. "If I broke even when you were the only one winning, I must have done something right."

"No, you were just lucky. If we'd played longer, I'd have cleaned you out, too."

Merle Hollister put the deck down. "You know, Clay, I think I might have known your mother."

Clayton stared, astonished.

"Did you come from Virginia?" the gambler asked.

The young card player hesitated. He'd tried to keep his ancestry, or anything personal, just that. Private. Still, if this gambler fellow, unlikely as it seemed, could have somehow known his mother, Clay wanted to hear about it.

"Never knew either of my parents," he said softly. "I grew up in an orphanage in Richmond. In the confusion when the city fell to Union forces, I ran away. I've taken care of myself ever since."

The gambler was looking at Clay in a different way than he had all evening.

"How old were you when you left the orphanage?" Hollister asked.

"Thirteen."

A brief flash shot through the gambler's eyes, brown like Clayton's, but darker and deeper.

"How can a thirteen-year-old manage alone? You must have had some hard times."

Clayton's head came up proudly. "I was a damned good rebel. I was going to join up and help the South win the war. Then Lee surrendered before I found an outfit that would take me. I fell in with a couple of fellows going home to Texas."

He paused to let out a sigh. "I didn't find out until much later that the horse they gave me was stolen from a Yankee captain. This pair kept telling me how great it was to be from Texas and how when we got there I could work on their father's ranch."

Clay considered everything he was *not* saying, but continued. "Only when we got to their place, it was abandoned. The buildings were falling down. They looked around for a long time and finally found their younger sister living with a distant cousin."

"And what did *you* do?" Merle Hollister demanded.

"That's when I helped a bunch of young fellows round up cattle to take to market. We took everything we could get hold of, whether it was branded or not. The fellow running things said he'd pay over to the different ranchers whatever their cattle brought. The rest of us could split the money from the unbranded longhorns."

The gambler raised an eyebrow. "But . . . ?"

"Trouble was, those ranchers waited until we'd done all the work. Then they came in and took over. Told us to get lost. Well, they had more men and more guns, and we were out."

Clayton felt Hollister's gaze and tugged at his suddenly tight shirt collar. Feeling more than a little sheepish, he went on with his story.

"The next year I signed on with an outfit to help drive a herd to Abilene. I've not been back to Texas since. I've worked on helping build the railroad, and I rode shotgun for a small stage line. When I came here to Agate I was driving a freight wagon. So I might not have much experience playing poker, but I've done plenty other things."

Clayton took a deep breath. He thought he'd said more than he ever meant to and hoped that now Merle Hollister would explain how he might have known the younger man's mother. But as several quiet seconds passed, Clay couldn't stand to wait.

"You knew my mother, then? I'd like to hear about it. But I don't see how you possibly could have, when I never knew her myself."

Another long silence ensued. Clayton was about to burst it when Hollister finally said, "I guess I've always been a gambler of one kind or another. Before the war I traveled a lot, buying cotton for a mill in New England. I met a lot of people in the South."

Clayton held his tongue while the man in black flicked a long look over him.

"There's something about you, like I'd known you or someone in your family before. Then, too, there's your name. Clayton. I got to know a family with that particular name very well."

"You two over there," the bartender suddenly boomed. "How about finishing so I can lock up and go home?"

Hollister momentarily stiffened, then put on the indifferent poker face he'd worn most of the evening.

He gestured. "You've got a small poke there, Clay. Want to cut the cards one more time for what's showing on the table?"

Around his shock at their previous conversation, Clayton shrugged. The gambler took it for agreement and pushed his stack of coins into the center of the table without counting. Clayton added all that were in front of him, then turned up a queen of diamonds. Hollister cut the deck, drew, and showed his ten of spades.

Silently, Merle Hollister stood up, walked over to the bar, and ordered one last brandy for the night. Clay pocketed the coins and went to the bar for a final word with the gambler. But the man's stiff back let Clayton know the last had already been spoken. Clay turned and left the saloon.

Chapter Two

****

"I should have looked the other way," Sid Ryder sneered through his week-old beard as he shoved Clay into the first of two cells. "If I'd turned my back long enough to have a smoke, the boys in the posse would have strung you up, and I wouldn't have another prisoner to bother with."

"Yeah. Makes no difference that I'm innocent." Clayton's voice rumbled with emotion. He went on, "I told you and *told* you I never killed any helpless old man. The money you stole out of my wallet I won playing poker last night."

"Sure, sure," the narrow-shouldered, hatchet-faced deputy replied. "I already heard that song. Only trouble is, the jasper you claim to have won the cash from ain't no place to be found."

Ryder slammed the heavy door and continued talking through the bars. "Clayton, I'm goin' to be rid of you once and for all. The circuit judge is due here tomorrow along with my boss, Sheriff Broward. When they hear the evidence against you, His Honor won't have no choice but to let me hang you."

The deputy stopped just short of a leering grin before he shrugged and turned to leave.

In despair, Clay yelled after him. "That gambler must have taken the morning stage. A rider on a good horse could catch him at the Dry Creek Station. He'd have to spend the night there."

Now Sid Ryder turned back with a real grin. "You know, Clayton, it does my heart good to have you crawl. So go ahead and cry. But I ain't goin' to send some puncher off on an all-night ride at county expense when it'll all come out the same either way."

The man in the cell called after the departing deputy, "I tell you, the man would back me up."

But Clayton realized the lawman was not going to hear anything he didn't want to hear. The prisoner stood looking through the bars at the closed door that led to the front of the jail building. The realization that he might really hang the next day almost overwhelmed him at first. But his despair gradually turned to a mature, tough optimism. Clayton made up his mind that he wouldn't be in his cell when the judge got there the next day.

He started by studying over where the walls and floor joined but found nothing that would help him. Then as he raised his head to look higher, he made contact with the coldest and hardest pair of gray eyes he had ever seen.

"So you claim to be innocent," the man in the next cell mocked. "Ain't none of us guilty, neither. We're pure as the driven snow, ain't we, boys?"

A hoarse answering laugh came from deeper in the cubicle as he continued, "But that judge'll be here come morning. More'n likely we'll all swing, and you right along with us hardened criminals."

Clayton squinted past the speaker. "Who are you? And how many of you are locked up in the same cell?"

Past the one who'd spoken to him, Clayton could see a large man sitting on a bunk, his features undistinguishable in the gloom. A third stood with his back turned, looking out the window.

"I'll do the honors," the first man said. "You must of heard of the Rome boys. I'm Jack Rome. The big one is Ty Rome, and the talky one by the window is Orville Rome."

"Yeah," the large man agreed as he got up. "Now we all been introduced proper and can travel to hell together."

"I'm Clayton. Most folks call me Clay."

He clumsily stuck his big right hand through the bars. The cold-eyed little man ignored it, but the large fellow came forward and grabbed Clayton's hand.

"Don't mind Jack," he said as he shook his dark curly head. "He's just naturally mean. Would rather pick a fight than anything else I know of. Fact is, none of us'd be here if he wasn't so anxious to shoot. When he's got a gun, more often than not he ends up killing somebody. If he ain't got anything else, he shoots off his mouth."

Jack whirled as if to attack the speaker.

Ty said to him, "Now, you know if you got no weapon, I can tear you up in little pieces."

Clayton barely noticed the interchange, intent on his own thoughts. He asked, "Have you looked this place over? I got no intention of being here in the morning when the judge gets to town."

"What do you think, we're stupid?" Jack snarled. "Of course we looked. There ain't no way out. You're just wasting your time."

But Clayton went on looking closely at every crack, every seam in the walls and floor.

The new voice, the third man's, sounded more intelligent. "Let him look. He just might find something we didn't. Besides, we couldn't check out *his* cell."

Clayton glanced over his shoulder. "Thanks. I generally do what I want, anyhow."

This third man, he saw, was average any way you looked at him. In height, Orville stood between the other two. Matter of fact, he was so ordinary he looked like a businessman. He was more than half bald and the least likely criminal Clayton had ever seen. He broke off his search as Orville stepped forward to speak to him.

"Since Jack and Ty have said so much already, you might as well know the rest. I don't suppose you've ever heard of us, but we all three rode with Chunk Colbert. We did just fine until Chunk got to thinking he was the fastest gun around. He called a fellow out who shot faster and straighter. Since that time I've been trying to run this outfit. But I'm not in Chunk's class, and we got caught."

Clayton tried to remember what he'd heard of an outlaw named Chunk Colbert, reported to be a fast gun who was suspected of a large number of crimes. But Orville Rome was speaking again.

"It sounded to me like the deputy wanted you out of his way."

Clayton thought about it a minute while he continued to look for an opening, no matter how small. Then he figured, why not? He told the Rome brothers how a young lady named Mary Ward had been Sid Ryder's girl until Clayton came to town and how now she'd been spending her time with Clay instead of the deputy.

Jack started to sneer a retort, but Clayton shut him up. He'd seen a crack in the ceiling that appeared a little different from the rest. Clay dragged his bunk underneath it and climbed up to look. Nothing much, but it was all he had. One of the ceiling boards was a quarter of an inch short and didn't butt tightly against the next.

Clay jumped down and rolled the thin pad that served as a mattress off onto the floor. He looked the frame over. It was wooden and cheap, put together with as few nails as possible. Turning it over to check the bottom, he searched for a nail that wasn't all the way in—or for anything he might work loose. What he found was a piece of flat metal an inch-and-a-half wide by eight inches long screwed to the bottom to hold a break in the two-by-four rail.

Clayton removed his belt. Using the edge of his large, flat buckle as a screwdriver, he soon had the metal strip off. He looked at Orville, his brown eyes dark and intense.

"What time do meals come around here?"

"Well, supper's next. It varies. Never before dark, and sometimes not until late."

"That doesn't tell me much. I got maybe an hour until dark. Listen, if you'll warn me when somebody's coming, I'll take all three of you out with me."

"You've got a deal," Orville said, with a chorus from both his brothers added on.

Orville Rome went to the window, where he could watch the path to the front door. Clayton jumped onto the bunk. Reaching as high as he could, he inserted the piece of metal into the small crack. Clay was surprised at the ease of his task. The first nail came loose with a screech, and a piece of wood an inch thick and six inches wide by four feet long fell down. Clayton almost dropped it in his excitement. He bent over and carefully put it down on the bunk.

Then he went to work in earnest, and soon he had an opening big enough to get his body through. But before he tried, he got down and took the boards he'd pulled off the ceiling and put them in a neat pile in the corner where his bunk had stood. He got back onto the bunk and reached up through the opening he'd made.

Clay couldn't quite get a handhold on the heavy beam. He jumped, and his fingers slipped along the wood.

"Damn!" he groaned out loud as he picked up a large sliver.

He got down. Using the edge of his belt buckle, Clay managed to pull the sliver out of his flesh, then tried once again to get through the opening. He used all the power in his legs to propel his body upward. The fingers of his right hand hooked over the edge, and he managed to hold his weight.

Willing his fingers to do the job, Clay raised his body enough to get his left hand over the top of the beam, and he soon had one elbow hooked over. He pulled and squirmed until he sat on the beam and waited there until he caught his breath.

The gable was dark and hot. All the heat of the day had been caught up where he was, between the roof and the ceiling. As his eyes got used to the gloom, he could make out that the joists the ceiling boards were nailed to were not uniform. Some were only a foot apart, while others were more than twice that distance.

Clay knew he could step only on the joists. If he put his weight on the boards, his foot might go through the ceiling. He dared not tempt fate that way. The second hole he made in the ceiling, Clayton reckoned, would have to let him down in the jail office. He moved very carefully to the front of the building. Then, when he was sure he was over the room where keys and guns were kept, he started in on the ceiling boards again.

Working from above was easier. In fact, it was almost too easy. The first board Clay pushed on nearly went right down into the office below. He barely caught it. Twisting the piece and getting hold of the end, he pulled it up through the hole where it had been fastened. Clay tried again and heard something hit the floor. A nail, by the ring.

God! he shouted in silence. If Sid came back and saw that nail on the floor, the whole plan would go up in smoke.

He had just laid the second board aside when he heard a loud hiss from the cell below. Clayton hurried toward the opening where he'd come up. His foot missed the joist, thumping hard against the ceiling boards. Something gave, but he managed to pull his weight back.

God! he thought again frantically. If he fell through now when someone was coming . . .

Clay heard an insistent hiss, and he slid through the opening. When the deputy walked in, the newest prisoner was lying on his bunk in the corner over the pile of boards, trying not to breathe too hard. It was soon obvious that Sid Ryder had come back to gloat.

"Clayton, I just know you'll want to hear this. I went to see Mary; I thought she should be informed on what a rotten polecat you turned out to be."

Sid held a rusty nail in his hand, turning it over slowly from time to time. Clay wished he could get his hands on the man and wipe that smug smile off his face. But he forced himself to say nothing and just wait.

The deputy soon went on. "I made sure I told Mary everything, about how you killed a helpless old man just to get a few dollars." Ryder waved the nail as he talked. "Oh, by the way, I'm tryin' to get her to come and watch me hang you."

His coarse laughter filled the jail as Clay came off his bunk and grabbed the bars.

"Sid, you're a lying son of a bitch." Clayton's voice shook, and the color drained out of his face. He finished in a whisper, "You'd better make sure you *do* hang me. Because if I was to get out of here alive, I'd come looking for you. Then I'd kill you real slow, like I hear some Indians do."

The two men stared at each other through the bars, their hatred filling the room. Sid Ryder dropped the nail he'd been holding and paid no attention to it. He stepped back a pace, looked at Clay another long minute, then turned and left.

Orville Rome's voice brought Clayton back to the present. "I think you'd best wait till after the deputy brings our supper before you work anymore on those ceiling boards. Then when we make our break we'll have all night before anybody starts to look for us."

Clay turned to look at him. "Right. I'm so close to breaking through to the office, I could do it in no time. But I *do* have to be sure nobody comes in before I'm ready." He stopped to ponder, then said, "Come to think of it, we need to make some plans. Are we going to ride away together, or should we each go our own way?"

Orville spoke up quickly without consulting his brothers. "We three always stick together, of course. You can come along if you want. It appears you're as much an outlaw as we are, like it or not."

Clayton thought about it. He'd never been on the wrong side of the law before. Oh, he'd been a little careless with a catch rope a time or two, but nothing to make him an outlaw. Anyhow, that was way down in Texas. What he really needed was to find that gambler and prove his innocence.

He said, "When we get out I'm riding south to Dry Creek Station to see if I can find the man I won the money from last night."

Jack Rome spoke with the same growl Clay had heard before. "You ain't never going to find the fellow. You might just as well admit what you are and ride the outlaw trail with us."

Clay's answer came back quick and clear. "No. I *have* to find him." Another thought came to his mind. "Where are your horses? I know the deputy left mine at the livery. Wouldn't surprise me if that damned Sid Ryder wasn't thinking to get hold of my buckskin once he gets rid of me."

The big man, Ty, spoke like there was no doubt Clayton would be riding with them from now on. "We all will ride whatever's handy. Fact is, we wouldn't of got caught, only the cayuses we were on gave out. The posse came up on us before we found a hole."

Jack finished for him. "We'll just take the best-lookin' mounts at the hitch rail along the street."

Clay shook his head. "It's no wonder you got caught. What you need is horses that won't be missed for a while. At least that way you might have more time before they start looking for you."

Feeling the brothers' eyes on him, Clayton said, "I know this town. I've lived here three months. What you should do is get your mounts from the second corral behind the livery. Alf Billings keeps the best horses in this part of the country there. That's where I expect to find my buckskin. He'd fit right in with that bunch."

Clay glanced up at Jack Rome and saw an ugly, yet knowing, grin come over him.

"Sounds like you got it all planned out," Rome observed.

Clayton stared him down, then said, "I'll take the half-broken three-year-old gray I'm buying off Alf. He'll spell my buck. That way, if that gambler has already left Dry Creek Station, I can keep going after him without exhausting the buck. You three ought to do what I said. If you're chased, you'd have an advantage over the law."

Jack spoke up. "But it don't make no sense. It would take too long to change mounts. Any posse I ever seen would gain too much while you was changing from one horse to the other."

Clay again shook his head. "You do whatever you want once we clear town. Till then, you either do what I say or stay here and wait for the judge."

Jack Rome snarled, "Just who in hell do you think you are, tellin' us what to do? We been in the business some little while, and here you come along, still wet behind the ears, but trying to take over. I'll bet you ain't never even killed a man."

Clayton merely looked at him. "Then stay in here. It makes no difference to me."

"Jack," Orville said beseechingly. "Just for once, keep quiet. You're always either shooting at people or shooting off your mouth. If you don't want to take advantage of Clay's offer, why, Ty and I working together could bind you up and gag you while we go out with Clay. In fact, he'd be a lot more use to us than a fellow who can't keep his trap shut or his gun in leather. Now, what's it going to be?"

Clayton was surprised at Orville's show of authority. Jack must have been, too, for his mouth flew open. Then, when he *did* try to answer, all he could do was sputter and squawk. He finally gave in, resentment thick in his voice.

"Have it however you want. Once we get out of here, it'll be best if I just go my own way."

Jack Rome went over to the bunk and flopped down to stare up at the ceiling. Ty and Orville would be better off without their gunman brother, Clayton thought to himself. He turned to talk to Orville.

"You might not agree with me. But I'm sure you'd get a lot farther with two horses apiece, even if it *does* take a couple of minutes to change saddles."

"I know you're right. I just wonder why neither Chunk Colbert nor I ever thought of it. Reckon Ty and I'll ride south with you as far as that station where you expect to find your gambler. From there it's only a short ride over to the state line. We're less well known there than hereabouts. Lawmen are a lot farther apart there, too."

Clayton refrained from showing his reaction. But it was obvious to him that, even after being caught, these Rome boys hadn't learned anything. Well, it was none of his business. Still, if he hadn't already promised, he knew now he wouldn't have taken them out when he went. However, if he didn't find the gambler, he'd most likely find himself in the same boat where they were.

Orville said, "There's a town over there. If you got a good stake you could lay low for a while, and they wouldn't turn you in."

Clay studied him. "Pardon my curiosity, but have you got that kind of poke?"

"Well, no, not at the present. But I think I might know a way to get what we need with some to spare."

Clayton quickly held up a hand. "I don't want to hear the details. All I'm interested in is getting out and finding that gambling man. Merle Hollister."

He broke off talking as someone came in the front door. The key worked in the connecting door. The bartender from the saloon came in, wearing a stained apron and bearing food. He was followed by the deputy. Sid Ryder drew his six-gun and held it in his right hand, while he unlocked the cell door with his left. The barman set the tray of food down just inside, then backed out and waited while Ryder locked Clayton's door and opened the other.

Clay ignored the proceedings until after the saloonkeeper left. Then the aroma of his dinner floated over to him, and he realized he was hungry. But he still didn't move.

"If it was up to me," the deputy said, "I wouldn't waste good vittles on any of you. Why feed somebody who's bound to hang soon?"

He watched a minute or two. When he got no response, Ryder laughed and went out, locking the connecting door on his way. Only then did the inmates move to pick up their meals.

"Bastard," Jack Rome growled after the deputy. "I'd like to teach him some manners."

Clayton cleaned off his plate without paying much attention to what he ate. When he finished he set the empty tray on the floor and turned to the men in the second cell.

"If two or three of you ride south with me, we'll do things my way."

Jack began his snarl, but Clayton cut him off. "Like I said before, it makes no difference to me. Only thing is, before we make the break I'd like to know what to expect."

He told himself he must be crazy even to *think* about traveling with criminals. As he occupied his mind pondering the possibilities, he lost awareness of time passing. After a while the outer door opened, and Clayton expected to see the bartender coming back for his trays. Shock pulsed through him when the one person he didn't want to see him behind bars walked in ahead of the deputy. Sid Ryder opened the second cell first, and Mary Ward removed the three trays. Then she turned to Clayton's cell and could barely keep her eyes off Clay while Ryder opened the door. She bent gracefully, picked up the tray, and placed it on the floor in the corridor. Mary glanced at the deputy and spoke with careful control in her voice.

"Sid, leave me alone with Clay for a minute."

Ryder's expression showed his disbelief. "Mary, it wouldn't be proper."

The girl never took her eyes off Clayton. "Please. This one time, do something because it's what *I* want."

"But he's charged with murder. It's not safe."

"How could it not be safe? The door is locked, and you've got the key."

Ryder's face sagged as if he were weakening. But he said, "If anything happens to you, I'll lose my job."

Mary's bright blue eyes flashed in her pale, delicate face. "And if you don't, you'll lose any chance of ever taking me anywhere again."

Ryder let out a long sigh. "Well, just for a minute. But I can't see why you'd want to talk to a killer."

"Clay is not a killer. At least not until he's had a trial and been found guilty."

Mary's golden red curls bounced emphatically as she advanced on the deputy. "Go on back to the office. I'll be all right."

Sid moved away reluctantly. "You sing out if he tries anything, and I'll come running. I'll be just through this door."

He left it open a crack behind him. Mary Ward followed him, closed it, then turned back. But the look on her face brought no good news, and her first words for him confirmed it, no matter what she'd said to Ryder.

"Clay, how could you murder a helpless old man?"

He stared at her. "How can you think that, Mary? You just said to Ryder that I've not yet been found guilty."

"I know," she said, sighing. "It's just that I want you to get decent treatment up until the end. And, well, you know how Sid can be with that mean streak of his."

"Mary." Clayton's brown eyes glittered with intensity. "I didn't kill that old man they found murdered."

He walked away to the far side of his cell, then turned back to the girl. "I never even knew somebody'd done in an old sodbuster till Sid got the drop on me, then said he was arresting me for the murder of a fellow I'd never met."

Mary just glared at him, and it was as if Clayton could read her thoughts.

He said, "I know, you're like Ryder. You think that because I had money on me when he took my wallet at gunpoint, I could only have gotten it by doing something awful. Well, I never killed any helpless person, and I never will. I won that money playing poker."

"Oh, sure," Mary answered with disdain. "How do you expect anybody to believe that? The whole town of Agate knows what a poor cardplayer you are."

Mary turned on her heel, stopping to pick up the empty trays on her way to the jail office.

Clay sank onto his bunk with his head in his hands. It was the final blow, he thought. Mary Ward had been his girl. How could she turn on him so quickly? And if she didn't believe him, who would?

He turned the situation over and over in his mind, trying to find some answer that would clear him. Well, the only way, he knew, was to catch up with the gambler he'd won the money from.

Clayton finally lifted his head. He looked around. The office door was closed. Almost no light came through the high window across the corridor. Then, suddenly, he listened hard. Someone was coming. He stretched out on the bunk and pretended to be asleep.

Sid Ryder came in, checking each cell door. He said in a loud voice, "Hey, high roller. Wake up and talk to me. Tell me one more time just how you won that money. Come on, wake up. What cards were you holding?"

Clay came to a sitting position, warily. He knew there was no use trying to tell it again and that Sid must want something else.

"Well, lover boy," the deputy sneered. "I see once you're behind bars you can't turn Mary's head like you always done before. Don't mind tellin' you, I was a little scared lettin' you and her talk without me being there. But it turned out better that way."

Clay held his tongue, refusing to add to Ryder's pleasure in any way. The silence didn't last long.

Sid said, "Now, after I've got you hanged, I won't have no trouble convincin' her to marry up with me."

His harsh laughter hung in the air after he went out. Clayton leaped to his feet and shook the cell door with all his might until he slid to the floor in a heap of exhaustion. Orville Rome's calm voice came as a shock to him, and Clay realized he'd forgotten the three in the other cell.

Orville said, "The deputy won't be back tonight. This was what he calls his bed check. I don't know what he does late at night, but he's never come back afterward."

Clayton looked over to the second cell, quieting his ragged breath. Then, without a word, he got up and slid his bunk under the hole he'd made in the ceiling. In a matter of minutes he swung himself up to the crawl space in the gable and finished breaking through the ceiling where he could get down into the jail office. He jumped.

In the gloom Clayton could barely make out the desk and chair. He had to move carefully but was rewarded by finding his own six-gun and belt hanging from a wall peg behind the desk. The gun didn't feel right, though. He swung the cylinder out and felt it was unloaded. Finding a box of .45s in the third drawer on the right side of the desk once he'd searched a bit, Clayton loaded his gun and dumped the rest of the shells into his left-hand shirt pocket.

He was about to shut the drawer when something else there caught his eye. Wrapped in a small cloth bag, the contents of which he quickly shook loose and counted, was the exact amount of money he'd won in the poker game. Clayton stared at his windfall a moment, then stuffed it back in the poke and pocketed the whole thing.

Taking the key ring from the nail beside the door, he went

to open the Rome brothers' cell. Then Clayton hesitated. Did he want to let three criminals out to prey on honest people? Well, dammit, why not? he thought with a flash of anger. After all, he very well might have to steal from now on.

He shrugged and turned the key. The first thing he heard was a complaint from the swarthy little gunman.

"It's about damned time," Jack Rome snarled.

The fellow's attitude gave Clayton second thoughts about what he was doing. Still, he wanted to free the other two. Without a word, he went back to the jail office.

Jack's voice followed him. "Goddammit, you come back here and let us out!"

When he got no response, he threatened, "By God, if you don't open this door, I'll holler so loud that somebody will hear and come to find out what the trouble is. Then you'll be—"

He stopped when Clayton returned to the cell block and walked to the door of the second cell.

"All right, loudmouth," Clay said quietly. "Turn around and back up to the bars."

"What the hell? Why should I?" Jack sputtered.

"Because that's the only way you're going to get out."

Clayton looked at the others. "You two want out bad enough to go without Jack?"

The pair exchanged a quick glance before Orville spoke. "For what it's worth, I'd rather not. But if it's the only way—"

He let it hang there. The gunman turned and stepped backward until he was within inches of the bars.

"That's far enough," Clayton ordered. "Now, put your hands behind you."

Jack Rome tried to look behind his back but couldn't see anything in the darkness. Especially not the handcuffs that Clay had gone to the office for and now reached through the bars and snapped onto Jack.

The gunman exploded with a series of oaths and comments on Clay's ancestry. Clayton let him go until he paused for breath.

Then he said in a cool tone, "Now, you can give me your word to keep your mouth shut, or you can stay behind. Just make up your mind. Which will it be?"

Jack turned around, somewhat subdued. "You win for now. Let us out. I'll keep shut till we're away."

With a touch of reluctance, Clayton opened the door. He led the way to the office and told Orville where the guns had been hung and where more shells could be found in the desk drawer. While they strapped on their weapons he went to the front door, opened it a crack, and watched the street.

Seeing nothing, Clayton said over his shoulder, "One of you, take Jack's gun and belt. We'll give it to him the first time we stop to blow the horses."

Jack Rome forgot his promise and couldn't keep quiet. "If you stop to fool around thataway, we won't get far."

Clayton stopped dead behind Jack and untied the man's bandanna from around his throat.

Before the gunman could finish spitting out "What the hell?", Clay pulled the neck scarf into Rome's mouth and tied it in a hard knot.

"If you can't shut up like you agreed on, we'll just help you," he said.

Ty took the way Clayton controlled his brother with a grin that showed how much he enjoyed the whole thing. But Orville's look was one of deep concern as he expressed the hope that Clayton knew what he was doing. Clay's answer was to open the door to the street and lead the way down along the dark side of the building.

"Just follow me. One of you, stay behind Jack in case he causes trouble."

At the livery barn Clayton stopped in front of Jack. "If I take the gag off, will you stand in the shadows and keep watch while we rope out the best mounts?"

He could almost feel the gunman glaring at him. But all

Jack Rome did was nod his head. Clayton untied the bandanna and shoved it into Rome's back pocket.

"Don't make a sound unless somebody's coming," he ordered.

Jack leaned forward and said under his breath, "Bastard."

Clayton tensed momentarily but chose to ignore the challenge. He found his own saddle on a rack of saddles and took his catch rope from it. Going on to the second corral, he began to rope out mounts, two for each man, knowing if the horses whinnied much, they were all as good as dead. For himself, he got his own buckskin and put a halter on the gray three-year-old, then tied him behind his saddle.

When they were ready to leave he asked, "Which one of you has got Jack's gun?"

"I do," Orville answered.

Clayton said, "I'll trade you the key to the handcuffs for his iron. That way he won't be shooting me in the back."

"I sure as hell don't need to backshoot a greenhorn like you," Jack Rome growled.

In response, Clayton merely held out the key toward Orville, and the exchange was made. Clay hung the belt and six-gun over his saddle horn.

"Walk your horses until we're well out of town," he directed.

Chapter Three

****

A pair of long hours later, Clayton pulled the tired buckskin behind an outcropping of rocks and started to change his saddle to the gray. Orville and Ty followed his lead and went right to work changing to their spare mounts. But Jack set his wet, tired horse and watched.

When Clay hung the gunman's belt and weapon over a nearby rock, Jack reined his mount over between Clay and the gun. Then he got down, took his belt and six-gun, and buckled up.

"It's not loaded," Clayton announced calmly.

Jack snarled back, "No, you ain't got the guts to let me load it."

Clayton sighed. "I guess you'll not be satisfied till one or the other of us is dead. Well, I don't see it that way. If I prove to you that I can draw faster and shoot straighter, will you agree to do things my way?"

Jack Rome's laughter held no humor. "Ain't no way to prove that, 'ceptin' with lead."

Clayton turned to the others as he opened the cylinder of his six-gun and shook out the shells.

"Ty. I want you to give the signal. Orville will judge which of us pulls the trigger first on an empty chamber."

"Sure," Ty agreed promptly.

But Orville stood shaking his head. Finally he said, "Oh, all right. You two, stand facing each other about ten feet apart. Ty, don't you signal until a time after each one says he's ready."

"This is ridiculous," Jack complained. "But go ahead whenever this pilgrim claims he's set."

Clayton stood, relaxed, as he looked at his opponent. Jack Rome had sunk into a crouch with his right hand claw shaped over his holstered gun.

"Ready," Clay said.

Orville spoke up, his voice loud in the quiet night. "I ain't goin' to say nothing, just to make it fair. It'll be the first sound you hear after I'm done talkin'. That there gray of Clayton's has been pawing kind of impatient-like. The next time his hoof hits the ground, go."

Seconds crawled by. Clay could feel the other man's tension. He wondered, Was Jack's ego so out-of-bounds that he'd wind himself up tight for a contest he said wouldn't prove anything?

Jack shifted his stance and expelled a long-held breath. Clayton felt the gray move. A second before its hoof hit, Clay's hand scooped the .45 out of leather. Jack Rome's arm stretched down, came back up. His gun was almost level when Clayton pulled the trigger. No need for Orville to make a judgment. Everyone there heard the sound of Clayton's hammer hitting the firing pin.

Jack never pulled at all. He turned aside, muttering, "It'll be different when we both know there's lead for the slow one."

Clay loaded his six-gun. When he pulled the cinch tight on his saddle, he looked across to see Orville and Ty off to one side in private conversation. He mounted, picked up the lead of the buck, and rode out—not caring if any of the three went with him or not.

The gray was anxious to prove itself, and Clayton, in a foul mood, let it out. He'd covered a couple of miles when he thought to pull the horse down to a slower gait. Then he realized that both Ty and Orville were only a few yards back, keeping pace. The threesome rode down the stage road without a word. Both outlaws seemed content for Clayton to lead. He never looked back to see if Jack Rome was coming, nor did he notice whether Jack's brothers did.

Sometime after midnight the road took a swing to the right and ran downhill to the relay station, halfway to Dry Creek. But Clayton held a little left and went off the road for the first time. In just a little way he led them over a small hill and down to a hidden spring. When he got there he let the buckskin drink while he pulled the saddle off the gray and rubbed it down with a handful of dry grass.

A pattern had already been established. Both Ty and Orville followed Clayton's lead, no matter that he was the youngest by far. When Clay felt the gray had cooled enough, he let it drink sparingly. Then he put the saddle back on the buckskin, mounted, and waited for the pair of outlaws to finish.

When they were in the saddle he said, "There'll be a few miles of rough going. Then we'll come back onto the stage road about six miles before the Dry Creek Station. If we time it right, we should be there before any of the passengers finish their breakfast."

Orville observed, "You seem to know this area pretty well. I thought I heard you say you'd only been in this part of the country for three months."

Before Clayton could answer, Ty said, "Yeah, you must of been through here before. You knew right where that spring was."

"No, I've never been over this part of the range."

"Then how did you know where that water hole was?"

"Well, I'll tell you. I've been over a lot of trails, and I've met a lot of travelers. When they talked, I listened. Once, a fellow I met at a saloon up in Montana told me about this hidden spring and how to find it if I ever came along this stage road and didn't want to stop at the relay station."

Ty stared in astonishment. "I'll be damned!"

* * *

The sun was halfway over the horizon when the trio sighted the barn and corral of the Dry Creek Station. Clayton pulled his mount down to a walk.

He asked, "Is there any chance either of you will be recognized by anyone down there at the station?"

Orville gave Clayton a surprised look. "I really don't think so. We've taken much longer chances."

"Might be you brothers need to figure the chances closer," Clay said. "When we get down there, we'll just be travelers wanting breakfast. Don't do anything to rouse anybody's suspicions."

Clayton jigged the buckskin into a lope and led the way to the front of the station. A hostler looked up curiously from his job, getting the stage teams ready for the next lap. The Concord sat just outside the corral.

Clay walked his mount up to the gate and asked, "How much for grain for our horses and some grub for the three of us?"

The young fellow brushed long, dirty blond hair out of his blue eyes with his fingers.

"Ain't got no grain to spare. Tie 'em at that rail aside of the barn, and I'll throw 'em some fodder. I'll rub 'em down soon as I get these'ns hitched. Stationmaster's inside, just go on in. They's set down to the meal already."

Clayton nodded to the other two, then turned back to the hostler.

"Did a man come in on the stage last night, about forty or so? Dressed like a gambler? You know, fancy vest and shirt, black coat and pants. Trimmed beard with streaks of gray in it?"

"Yeah, he come in. Didn't stay, though."

Clayton tried to keep from showing his disappointment. "I thought that stage stayed here overnight," he said.

"It does."

Without meaning to, Clay spoke in a loud voice. "Where

would he go next? It's important. I've got to talk to Merle Hollister."

"Mister, don't get upset with me," the horse handler protested, taking a short step backward.

Clayton ground his teeth inside clenched jaws. "How did the gambler leave? Which way did he go?"

"I don't know. How could I?" The hostler fidgeted, getting more and more nervous.

Clayton sighed and fought for control. He was becoming too agitated, he knew. He didn't want the kid to see how much, or to remember it too well later.

"I'm sorry. What's your name, by the way?"

"Most folks just call me Blondy. Ma give me a name everybody laughs at, so I don't use it much."

"Right. Well, then, Blondy, did somebody meet Hollister here with a horse? Or did he buy a horse from the station? Somebody around here must have seen which way he went."

"No, sir. That gambler fellow didn't do none of them things."

"But he didn't just walk away without being seen. How could he have disappeared into thin air?"

Blondy rubbed his palms together, then wiped the sweat onto his pants.

"There was this card game in the main room last night. Him and the station boss and some of the other passengers. They was going strong when I went to bed. This morning the gambler was gone and so was the boss's best saddle horse. Mr. McKenna—the boss—was fit to be tied. He couldn't go after the gambler, 'cause he had stage passengers to take care of." The hostler looked distracted. "Please, mister. Go talk to Walt McKenna. If I ain't got the teams ready when the driver wants to go, I'll lose my job."

He turned away and went back to harnessing the stage teams. Clayton looked across the porch to Ty and Orville Rome, waiting by the station door. He nodded and crossed to them, and they walked into the dining room.

* * *

From the outcropping of rock where Clay had stopped to change saddles the first time, Jack Rome watched his older brothers follow the newcomer down the stage road.

He muttered to himself. If only he had loads for his six-gun, he'd sure as hell show that young jasper up for trying to be the leader—and not even being dry behind the ears yet.

Jack stood there alone for a time. He hated the younger man who'd had the nerve to gag and handcuff him. Then his mind turned back to recalling where he could find shells for his .45. That third drawer down on the right side of the desk in the jail office in Agate!

If he staked the wet mount on some grass right here where he was and put the saddle on the fresh one, he could go back and get all the shells he needed. Then he could ride like hell, change the damned saddle again, and catch that bastard Clayton while he was still at the Dry Creek Station.

Jack's thought fathered his action. He soon had the saddle on the second horse and was spurring it back the same way they'd come. Having no interest in the well-being of his mount, he made even better time going back than he, his brothers, and Clayton had made riding away.

When he got to town, Jack Rome stopped at the same second corral behind the livery stable and traded the worn-out mount for the first horse he could put a rope on. Just as he tightened the cinch, he heard someone coming. Jack led the new horse through the shadows at the side of the building to the street.

He could hear a pair of men offsaddling in the stable, but he paid no attention. Rome thought only of his objective, waiting in the battered desk drawer in the jail office. Soon he reached the front door. He saw no light and walked boldly into the office and struck a match.

Jack spotted a lamp on the wall and held the fire to the wick. It took almost no time for him to find the shells and get his gun fully loaded.

As he finished, the door burst open, and Sid Ryder, the deputy, hurried in.

"Sheriff Broward, I didn't know you was—" He stopped cold and stared at Jack. "What the hell? You ain't my boss."

Sid went for his gun, a foolish mistake since the man behind the desk had his in hand. As the deputy got his right hand around the butt of his holstered iron, Jack shot him twice in the chest.

Killing didn't disturb Jack Rome. In fact, it made him feel more alive than at any other time. He bounded over the fallen lawman and took a quick look out the open door. Seeing no one, he closed the door and walked slowly back to the desk, thinking hard.

Now he knew a good way to fix that bastard Clayton, Jack decided. He searched for and found a wanted poster on the desktop, turned it over, and scrawled in a labored hand:

MARY,

FORGIVE ME. I ONLY DONE WHAT I HAD TO.

CLAY.

Then he dragged the body of Sid Ryder over and propped it in the chair behind the desk. He left the note on the desk right in front of the body. Jack reckoned it would look for all the world like Clayton had shot the deputy while he sat there, giving Ryder no chance.

Jack Rome left the jail office with the light on and the door ajar, muttering aloud, "That'll fix the young son of a bitch."

He mounted his third stolen horse of the night and rode for the outskirts of town. Halfway to the stable, Jack met a pair of men walking toward him. He gave them a wide berth, but even so, he couldn't help noticing that the slightly taller man had a star pinned to his vest. Jack Rome hurried down the stage road.

* * *

Sheriff Ted Broward turned to look at the rider leaving town at a time when most men were bedding down for the night. When he turned back he saw the light on in the jail office.

"Well, what do you know?" he said to his companion. "My deputy must be expecting me for once."

"I'm tired," the other, older fellow announced. "I think I'll go right to the hotel and get settled for the night. If you get away from your man anytime soon, I'll buy you a drink."

"Fair enough. I'm sure I'll be right along, Your Honor."

The pair parted company, and Broward went over to the jail. When he walked in, he forgot all about the offer of a drink. The first thought he had was of the man he'd seen riding out past him and the judge.

In the main room at the Dry Creek Station, Clay and the two Rome brothers were finishing a big meal. Clayton found himself watching the girl who served the food. He gathered she was the stationmaster's niece, and he heard Walt McKenna call her Betsey. She was a rather tall young woman, with shoulders a bit wider and more square than usual. Her face was somewhat long, too, and her jaw was strong. But when she smiled at him, Clayton thought she was almost pretty. She certainly stood straight and had beautiful shiny hair that was nearly black. And her hazel eyes twinkled when someone's talk interested her.

Clayton felt good about McKenna as well. He'd found it easy to converse with the stationmaster and had confided in him about being falsely arrested for murder and taking his own horses back from the livery in an attempt to catch up with the one man who could clear him. He only neglected to say where he had picked up his two followers.

Walt McKenna, who appeared grizzled and weathered more than his actual early middle age, said, "I'd sure appreciate it if you could bring my horse back. I hate worse than anything losing a good mount. That man might have cheated me in the poker game, but I've lost money playing cards before. It's the horse I need."

"Can't promise anything, but we'll sure try," Clayton said as he set his coffee cup down, and the two brothers nodded in agreement.

Clay went on to ask, "You have any idea as to which way a man would go from here on your stolen horse?"

McKenna scratched the stubble on his chin. "The most likely direction would be west to the state line. I've heard of a town someplace over there in the mountains where outlaws are supposed to hole up after they steal from us honest folks."

"Have you got any notion on how to find it?"

"No, I don't. I doubt any up-and-up man would. You know, son, you'd best leave it all be. You could go someplace else. Say, down to Arizona, change your name, maybe grow a beard. Chances are you could live a quiet life on some small ranch and nobody'd ever be the wiser."

Clayton began to shake his head, but the stationmaster went on. "Think about it, son. It'd be a whole lot better'n gettin' your neck stretched."

Betsey stood quietly behind the men, listening closely with a sympathetic expression as Clayton burst out, "No, by God! I didn't kill that old man they found murdered. I've never killed any helpless person."

But Orville Rome held up his hand for silence and turned his head. After a minute he said, "A rider is coming."

Ty got up and went out through the kitchen. Clayton's curiosity was piqued, and after only a minute or two, he went out onto the porch. He stood watching a small dust cloud move down the trail.

Clay heard someone behind him and said, "Whoever it is, he's sure punishing the horse." When he got no answer he continued, "You think Jack would . . . ?"

He turned with the unfinished question and was startled to realize he'd been talking to Walt McKenna and not Orville. Clayton shifted his gaze to the doorway behind them and was able to make out Orville standing in the shadows. Orville Rome was shaking his head, and Clay tried to figure out the message he sensed was being sent to him.

But the stationmaster responded to Clayton's *first* comment.

"Yeah, that yahoo is sure carrying the mail."

Clayton moved back to the shadows against the wall. It dawned on him that he shouldn't just show himself out in the open, at least not until he caught up with Merle Hollister and had things put to rights. Orville and even McKenna had taken care to see the rider before he saw them, and so had Ty by going out through the kitchen door at the side. No, Clay had to berate himself, he hadn't been thinking the way a decent outlaw would.

Now as he watched the rider approach, he saw that it was, indeed, Jack Rome. He sucked in his breath, not sure how he should react if the little gunman was on the prod. He figured Jack might well have found a way to get loads for his gun.

Jack didn't stop at the barn as his brothers and Clayton had. He brought his lathered, heaving mount to a sliding halt at the edge of the porch. Walt McKenna was visible in the sunlight there, and Jack started in with him immediately.

"I'm lookin' for three fellows, each leadin' an extra horse. They was headed this way when I seen 'em last night."

McKenna was cautious. "What do you want 'em for, mister?"

"It don't matter to you," Rome flared, his temper hot in a hurry, as usual. "Either you saw 'em or you didn't. Which was it?"

Clayton could see that the stationmaster was rubbed the wrong way by Jack's attitude. He knew something ought to be done before the gunman caused real trouble.

Stepping to the front of the porch, out in daylight, he asked, "Are you looking for me, Jack?"

Rome jerked and opened his mouth. But before he could say anything, Orville moved up from the front door and Ty came around the end of the station. Jack caught the movement out of the corner of his eye. He looked first at Ty, then at Orville. It didn't escape his notice that his own brothers now had him in a crossfire.

"What the hell?" he demanded. "Don't you trust me anymore?"

Orville answered, "Just playing it safe. Your temper being what it is, we thought to be sure of you."

Clayton didn't like considering what all Jack Rome might say in front of the stationmaster and decided to head him off.

"If you're hungry, there's probably enough left. You'd better eat if you're planning to ride with us."

Jack obviously wanted to say more. He struggled with it, paused, then finally shrugged.

"Yeah, I'll eat. And if you're headin' west, I'll go along."

He turned to Walt McKenna. "I need a horse. This'n ain't going to make it much further."

McKenna stiffened as he said, "Sorry. My best mount was stolen right out of the corral last night, and I can't spare any more."

He turned away in time to miss seeing the ugly look on Jack's face. Orville stepped down off the porch and started speaking very quietly to his brother. Clayton couldn't make out any words, but he gathered from the tone that Orville was trying to calm Jack down.

After a while Orville spoke to Clayton. "Go inside with Jack and rest while he eats. Ty and I will get the horses ready."

He picked up the reins for Jack's horse, but Jack Rome flared out again.

"I don't want this wet-behind-the-ears kid around. Let's take all the saddle stock and leave him. There's most like a lawdog after us by this time."

Clay whirled on Jack in anger, but Orville started speaking first.

"There's one thing you'd better know, Jack. Ty and I talked it over and decided that if you couldn't get along with Clay, you could split off in another direction. But we're staying with Clay. He's got a level head and won't get us into trouble."

Jack Rome made to protest, but Orville cut him off. "There's no use in talking. And if you're thinking to shoot Clay down, we've discussed that, too. If there's any gunplay between you two, Ty and I would both back Clay."

Clayton watched Jack struggle to master his disbelief. Then Clay said to Orville, "I aim to work a circle around this station and see if I can pick up any tracks. When I come back, let's get away from here."

He walked south on the stage road a short distance, studying the ground. All he saw were the marks of the Concord. There didn't seem to be any new or extra horse tracks, but he found it impossible to be sure. Then he went west to Dry Creek, which he saw was living up to its name. He crossed the creek and walked back north. When he was about even with the station, he found the west bank torn where McKenna's stolen horse must have scrambled up.

When Clayton was past the buildings, he cut back to the road they'd ridden in on. He already knew there were no tracks going back the way they had all come. After he'd made a complete circle, he returned to the corral. Ty was waiting with all the horses.

Clay noticed that the tired mount Jack had ridden was on a lead, and Jack's saddle was on Orville's extra horse.

"Everything ready?" he asked Ty.

"Yeah. Orville went in to get Jack."

Clayton turned and started toward the station. Without exactly knowing why, he felt desperate to get away from there. The thought of Betsey McKenna's smile came to him, and he decided to go to the back door and through the kitchen.

As he reached for the latch on the back door, it opened. Betsey stood there facing him. She stepped through and quietly closed the door. Standing right in front of him like that, she didn't look quite as tall as she had when she served the meal. Betsey spoke as if she knew there probably wasn't much time.

"Don't ride with those other men. Especially not the one who came in last, Clay." He looked so surprised that she continued. "I get a chill every time he looks at me. Maybe the other two are all right, but I really don't think so."

For some reason he didn't understand, Clayton felt he had to be straight with her.

"I don't trust Jack Rome, either. But I think you might be wrong about his brothers. They're outlaws, but neither would go against me."

Clayton reached out a hand toward Betsey as if to shake hers. She met it halfway, but before any more words could be spoken, they both heard a clatter of hooves.

Clay pulled his hand away, said "Good-bye," and ran back to the corral.

He made out Jack leaving to the west. He met Orville coming from the front and asked, "Do you think Jack knows something we don't?"

"I don't know. But it might be wise to get away, since he seems to be in such a hurry."

They swung into their saddles and rode west, covering any trail Jack Rome might have left.

Chapter Four

****

The three men, each leading an extra horse, rode hard until midafternoon. They changed horses twice and never caught up with Jack. Then suddenly they came to a small stream, and there he was, his saddle cinch loose, waiting for them. His first words proved he intended to take over as leader.

"We'll lay up here till sundown, then hide our tracks by ridin' in the water. We'll get to The Settlement after moonrise."

Clayton didn't want to have trouble with the gunman. He looked instead to Orville. "The Settlement?"

Orville nodded. "That's what the place we're going to is called."

He pulled the saddle off his mount and said to Clayton, "Jack knows the way better than Ty or me. I've only been there once. When we arrive you'll have to convince the boss or one of his top men that you really are on the run from the law."

Remembering something Orville had said earlier, Clay asked, "How are we going to pay our way? You said it was expensive."

Orville opened his mouth to answer, but Jack beat him to it. "The job we got figgered out should get us credit, as long as we agree to split it with the boss."

Clayton turned away, feeling trapped. He didn't want to be part of a robbery, or maybe even worse. Yet he knew he had to go on with these three. The law was most likely behind them by this time, and the only man who could clear him was headed toward this so-called Settlement. How in hell was he going to stay honest?

As if to leave him with his troubled thoughts, the rest of the trip went by in silence. Jack Rome led the way, first upstream, then over a rock ledge. Most of the time they kept the horses to a walk. Jack made them ride single file anytime he thought the ground would show tracks.

Even though Clay tried to keep track of landmarks, his journey was long and boring. Then once again they rode in a streambed, this one all rocks and with quite a pitch. The horses labored to get up. There was an armed guard between an inconspicuous pair of low hills. Clayton was relieved as they passed through. The fact that he was riding with known outlaws apparently got Clayton in. He wondered if he would ever come out.

Clay learned he'd passed only the first test. They weren't to The Settlement yet. After they rode for what seemed like at least another hour, they came to a place where they had to ride single file between standing rocks that towered above them. Afterward, thinking back, he reckoned the next challenge shouldn't have surprised him. But at the time he jerked on his mount's reins, then had to fight to regain control.

"Hold and sing out."

The voice was close. Only Jack, in the lead, took it in stride.

"Jack Rome."

"Pass. Next?"

"Ty Rome."

"Pass on, Ty. Next?"

"Orville Rome."

"Pass, Orville. Next?"

Clay's voice didn't quite work, and the guard spoke again. "Speak up quick or die."

"Clayton is my name. Clay, to most folks." He started his horse after the Rome brothers' mounts.

"Hold it. Ain't never heard of you. Talk fast or try to outrun hot lead."

"He's all right," Orville intervened. "They were getting a rope ready for him in jail. When he broke out, he took us with him."

The tone held no give, but the lookout said, "You'll have to take responsibility for him. That way he can get by till the man says different."

Clay heaved a sigh, then wondered how much had been solved. How soon would he have to prove himself again to somebody even harder and more demanding? He wanted to turn and run, but he knew he was trapped. Everything looked like it was against his attempt to stay honest, and he could see no way out.

He wondered if any other decent men were here in The Settlement, bound by circumstances. If there were, how could he find them? Even more, could he get them together to help one another? No, Clay told himself, he had to be daydreaming. Most likely there were none, and if there *were*, they'd been here awhile. They'd already be tarred with the outlaws' brush.

The horses finally finished their struggle to climb out of the streambed. Clay was relieved to find he could again ride beside Orville. At least Orville was a man who was known in this place, where everybody would turn against Clay if they suspected he was honest.

Orville Rome might have had some idea as to what Clayton was thinking, for he said, "Most likely nothing will happen tonight. But someday soon the man or one of his lieutenants will want you to prove that you belong here. I've heard they didn't used to be so hard to convince. Then one time not so long ago a lawman posed as an outlaw. Almost got away with it, but he was found out."

Clay glanced at the older man. "What did they do to him?"

"Way I heard it was, they broke both arms and both legs, then blindfolded him and turned him loose. A couple of days later somebody went out to make sure he was dead. Some say it was several miles away, and others say it wasn't far at all, but the lawman was found. He'd managed to get the blindfold off and was crawling along on his elbows. The fellow who found him took pity and put a forty-five slug in the back of his head."

The story did nothing to help Clay's state of mind, so he spoke no more. The four rode on, and shortly they saw a light ahead. They came up to a cluster of buildings. Those Clayton could see were made of logs, the largest of which appeared to be a saloon.

Jack was in the lead. He stopped off to one side and dropped his bedroll, then went to the saloon without saying anything. Orville and Ty dismounted and unsaddled. Clay did the same, except that he hobbled his two horses. Ty never noticed, but Orville shot a look at Clay, then shrugged.

Clayton quickly said, "I just feel better if I can get a mount in a hurry."

Orville nodded, and he and Clay unrolled their beds under the stars. Ty walked away toward the lights, saying, "I won't be long. Just a drink or two and I'll be back."

Clay tried to settle down but lay awake for what seemed like hours. Long after Ty returned and flopped on top of his blanket. But when he woke, it was morning, and the sun was in his eyes. He sat up and looked around. Ty and Orville sat at a small fire, eating the last of the supplies they'd brought from the Dry Creek Station. When Ty observed that Clayton was awake, he looked at his brother and then nodded at Clay.

Orville turned and said, "If you want anything to eat, Clay, you'd better get over here before Ty crams it all down his own throat."

Clay grinned and got some food. When he finished he asked, "What are we going to eat from now on?"

"There's a store here where you can buy what you need,"

Orville answered. "But it costs two or three times as much as what you'd be used to."

Clay said, "I'll kick in what I've got, but if the prices are that bad, it won't last long."

Ty spoke up. "Just as soon as Jack gets sober, we'll talk to the man in charge or one of his lieutenants. If he approves of our plan, we can get credit."

Clay sat around talking and drinking coffee with the two. It was midmorning before Jack finally came to their campsite and poured himself a tinful of coffee. He didn't say a word to the others, and they didn't try to talk to him.

He poured a second, then turned his head to stare at Clayton, almost as if he'd forgotten about him.

Jack Rome swallowed half his coffee and said, "A new fellow I don't know has got close to the man. Scuttlebutt has it nobody gets to the man unless they go through this fellow."

He downed the rest of his tinful as Orville asked, "Does this lieutenant have a name?"

"All I know is, I heard him called Stoney. Feller what told me says he's pure poison with a gun or knife."

"Don't make no difference," Ty stated. "We got to talk to somebody or else get out."

Clay's attention was distracted by a boy in his early teens coming across the grass toward them. When the boy began to hurry, he showed a noticeable limp. He looked them over one at a time, then settled on Clay.

"Stoney said you was to come. Now."

Clayton got to his feet. He glanced at Orville, who muttered, "Good luck."

Ty asked Clay, "How are you with your left hand?"

"OK," Clay answered, "but it's not quite the same as my right. Why?"

In answer, Ty Rome tossed him a six-shooter. "Here, take my extra."

Surprised, Clay nodded his thanks, tucked the gun under

his belt, and followed the newcomer toward the town. To cover his nervousness he asked, "What's your name, son?"

The fellow looked up, obviously taken aback at being spoken to. "They just call me Boy." He dropped his gaze to his boots, embarrassed.

Clayton's interest was piqued. "Hardly seems the sort of place for one so young. Don't you have any parents?"

When Boy didn't answer, Clay looked closer at him, finding fear on the thin face that was both old and young.

"Look here, son, I'm not about to do you harm. I'm just talking, trying to be friendly."

Still no response. Clayton ventured, "I'm new here and don't know the ropes. I'll bet you could tell me how to handle this fellow I'm going to see, so as not to get into trouble."

As Boy slowed, his limp disappeared. He took a quick glance at Clayton. "If he don't believe what you tell him, he'll have you thrown out. Or if he should think you was a lawman, he'd shoot you hisself."

Boy resumed his jerky gait. Try as he did, Clay couldn't get any more out of him. They walked along a dusty street, the few buildings standing spaced at irregular intervals. Clayton took particular notice, just in case he ever needed to get from one end of the single street to the other without being seen.

Midway along, they turned in at what appeared to be a small house. Boy went up the two steps to the door, ordering, "Wait here."

His knock was answered immediately by a man who looked like he could last several rounds with a grizzly. Boy spoke to the fellow. The large man looked hard at Clay, then turned and said to someone inside, "The one as came in with the Rome brothers is here and looks to be alone."

A new voice answered, "Tell him to wait."

The big man closed the door and turned back to the boy. "Get out." Then he told Clayton, "He ain't ready for you yet. Just wait here till he comes out."

The muscled, bald hulk walked to the corner of the house and leaned against the outside wall in the shade, watching Clay. After a minute Clay began to feel impatient. He had never gotten accustomed to being kept waiting. Clayton fidgeted, then looked toward the big man who merely stood and watched him. Clay almost spoke, then thought silently that this must be some kind of test and he'd better get himself under control. He turned his back and sat down on the steps, willing himself to wait quietly.

He couldn't have told how long he sat there with the sun hot on his back. When the door finally opened, Clay was almost surprised, but he kept calm. He rose slowly and turned.

The fellow had to be the one called Stoney, but he certainly didn't look like what Clayton had expected. Standing taller, two steps above Clay, he seemed bigger than he was. He had about ten years on Clay and looked like any businessman, except for the tied-down gun rig on his right side. His skin was soft and white, as if he never went out in the sun. A paunch hung over his belt.

Stoney spoke distinctly but quietly. "You're Clay."

Since it wasn't a question, Clayton merely nodded.

The fellow continued. "I hear you engineered a jail break in Agate."

Again, Clay only nodded. If he didn't speak, this Stoney might not know how scared he really was.

"Why'd you bring the Rome boys out with you?"

Clay could no longer avoid answering. "I wanted to leave Jack behind, but I'd made a deal with Orville."

"What were you in for?"

Clayton thought he couldn't tell the whole truth here. "They said I killed a man for his money."

Stoney turned to the big man at the corner, obviously not caring if Clay was innocent or guilty. "What do you think, Beef?"

The bald guard stepped out into the sunlight. "I think he

don't like waiting for anybody but can play it level when he has to."

Stoney turned back to Clayton. "Can you shoot?"

Clay shrugged deceptively. "Better than most, not as good as some."

Stoney looked again to the man he'd called Beef, and Clayton did the same. The fellow must have been ready. He opened his hand for a moment, and Clay saw five small stones.

Beef closed his hand and said, "Shoot." With an underhand motion he threw the stones into the air.

Clayton had played this game before. He scooped his .45 out of leather. Timing it just right, he fanned the gun five times. Four of the stones broke into fragments before the six-shooter's roar died away. Clay swung the cylinder open and shook out the used casings while watching Stoney.

Stoney's mouth quirked into a brief smile. "I see you've got a backup gun. How would you have done if you'd fired with your left hand?"

"I'm not as fast with it, but I'm as accurate," Clayton answered, his confidence restored by the good shooting. He didn't add that this was the best he'd ever done.

Stoney held his expression the same. "You can use this town. Buy whatever you can afford. If you have trouble with any of the men here, it'll be up to you to settle it between yourselves."

He started away, then turned back. "The place up there is off-limits."

Stoney gestured toward a large house uphill to the west, which Clayton couldn't have seen until the sun was well up. Stoney reached for the door, and Beef walked up the pair of steps to go inside with him.

Clay remembered that he was here to find the gambler who could clear him of murder. "Mr. Stoney?"

The man turned back, a different expression on his face. He waited.

"I'm looking for a gambling man," Clayton continued. "Dressed in black, about forty. Well-trimmed beard with some gray in it."

He noticed that a muscle twitched in Beef's face, but Stoney answered quickly. "Never did like the handle of Stoney. My name is Wall, if you're going to mister me. And we're all gamblers, one way or another. Only one we got here who dresses in black and wears a beard is Grover. You can almost always find him at the back table in the saloon."

After a short pause he added, "Grover keeps a sleeve gun, and he's mean."

With that he went through the door, and Beef was right behind him. The big bulk turned back at the last instant.

"He must like you; he don't let just anybody call him Stoney to his face," Beef informed Clayton.

Then his voice lowered and sounded threatening. "I think you're lucky, but I never trust lucky people. Luck changes."

As he slammed the door behind him, Clay stood considering. Somehow this Grover didn't sound like the man he was looking for. Well, what the hell? He had to pass the saloon on his way back to the Romes' camp, so he might as well make sure. Clayton also figured it was probably better for Stoney to like him than Beef, and he couldn't expect everybody to like him. After all, he wasn't running for public office.

Clay walked back the way he and the teenage boy had come. He noticed that now more men were out, up and down the street. Funny, he thought, it had seemed almost deserted coming the other way. He turned to go into the saloon.

As Clay entered he stepped to his left and waited. When his eyes adjusted to the gloom, he saw a rough plank bar along the left-hand wall. Even this early, a half-dozen drinkers were leaning on it. None paid any attention to him. He looked to the right and noticed several tables. A couple were round. One square table had three legs and a pile of boxes for the fourth. Against the right wall was a faro layout, and back in the far corner a poker game was in progress.

Clayton thought he had to look and act tough if he meant to survive in this place. He ambled down the length of the bar and looked carefully at each man. Most returned the favor, giving as good as they got. Clay crossed to the poker table and studied each player in turn.

When he finished, a fellow with his back to the corner said, "Purty good show. I wonder if you can back it up."

Clay didn't answer, so the man to the speaker's right stated, "He don't even look dry behind the ears to me."

Clay figured this one had to be Grover. He had a dirty beard and wore a grease-stained black coat over what once had been a fancy vest. His collar was open.

Clayton looked him in the eye. "Well, Grover, you can come see if you want. That is, if you're man enough."

He didn't worry about a fist fight with the scruffy poker player. Grover was a good six inches shorter and thirty pounds lighter than he was.

Grover raised his right hand to push his hat back. He said, "Big talk, sonny. I think you got a yellow streak running like a river right down your back."

His hand was still at his hat. Clayton ordered, "Either bring that sleeve gun out in the open so I can kill you or let your hand down slow and easy."

The gambler's hand inched down to the table. To save face, Grover said, "You're new here. I'll let you off this time, but don't cross me again."

Clay issued a brief, sardonic smile. He turned without saying more and slowly walked the length of the barroom. Clayton didn't look back. When he reached the street he turned right, not the short way to his camp. At the corner of the building he turned right again.

Clay dripped sweat. When he rounded the back of the saloon, a door opened just in front of him. Someone stepped out in his path. Startled, Clay drew his handgun without thinking and had it leveled before he recognized the young man who limped.

"By God, Boy, you should be more careful! A fellow could get shot by mistake if he steps out in front of a man that way."

"Sorry." The single word was so quiet, Clay almost missed it. With his head down, Boy asked, "Can I walk back to your camp with you?"

"Sure. Glad to have the company." As he spoke, Clayton realized the kid was accustomed to being abused and kicked around.

They walked along in silence until they were in sight of the camp. Then the boy said, without looking up, "Ma named me Henry, but Pa called me Hank."

"I guess you know I'm Clayton. Clay for short."

Hank nodded and said, "I'm glad Stoney liked you. Ain't many he'll help like he done you when he said to watch out for Grover's sleeve gun."

So Hank knew all this even though he'd been dismissed, Clay observed. Aloud he said, "Not any gladder than I am."

The thought came to Clay that Hank must know about all the men in The Settlement. He might have information to help Clayton find the gambler he was looking for. They stopped under an oak tree right out in the open, where they could be seen, but nobody would overhear what they said.

Clay asked, "Did you hear my whole conversation with Mr. Wall?"

Hank looked Clay full in the face for the first time. "Yeah, I was out of sight around the other corner from where Beef was."

"Then you know I'm looking for a gambling man."

"Yeah, but I ain't seen him around here. 'Course, I don't know 'em all."

Clayton tried to hide his surprise and disappointment. "But I doubt there are many you haven't seen, Hank."

"Just the man, I reckon, and two or three as live up on the hill with him."

Clay wondered out loud, "How long do you suppose a fellow would have to be here before he'd get a look at this man and his lieutenants?"

"No way of knowin'," Hank answered. "I been here since last fall, and I ain't never seen him."

"How did you happen to land here with this bunch of thieves and desperadoes?"

Hank couldn't seem to respond right off. His words finally came out sounding slow and controlled. "Ma died on the farm in Missouri where Pa was sharecroppin'. Him and me decided to come west and homestead, have a place of our own."

The boy stopped talking for so long that Clay was about to change the subject. But Hank took a deep breath and went on.

"Pa was in a hurry to get past the plains afore winter. He didn't want to wait for a regular wagon train, so we started out with a couple or so of freight wagons on their way to Fort Laramie. What we didn't know was that they was carryin' a large sum of money. We never had a chance. One of the other wagon drivers was workin' with the outlaws. He set us up, and when Pa and the others tried to fight back, they was all killed."

Hank paused awhile, rubbed his hip, and spoke again. "That's when I got shot. The lead is still in there and hurts like anything sometimes. I came to, lyin' on the ground. The wagons was all burning, and the outlaws was mountin' up to ride away. I didn't know I'd been shot, and I picked up a rifle and pointed it at one of 'em, but the durn thing was empty. Then one of 'em aimed his gun at me and hollered to the rest that he'd found one as wasn't dead yet. That was when a youngish fellow with 'em rode up and pushed this other'n's gun aside. He was leadin' an extra hoss and said for me to get on if I wanted to live."

Clay shook his head in wonder. "That's some story, Hank. Who was the fellow that saved you? Is he still here?"

Again, Hank looked down. "Naw. Grover shot him with that sleeve gun. I tried to stop the bleeding, like he done for me, but I couldn't save him."

Clayton and Hank sat under the tree for some time. They talked part of every day after that. Although Clay was several years older, they both knew they had become fast friends.

Chapter Five

****

Clay found it hard to accept the inactivity of living in a place like The Settlement. He was used to working or hunting for long hours. Clayton had admitted to himself a long time ago that he felt better when he kept busy.

His thoughts came back to the gambler, as they always did. Merle Hollister's trail had led to within a few miles of The Settlement. He must have come here, Clay reasoned. But if he had, where was he now? Try as he might, Clayton could find no trace of him.

There were but two ways in or out. The one Clay and the Rome boys had come in was guarded day and night. The other was up the canyon to the west and guarded by the large log house where the man and his lieutenants lived. That way was so narrow, Clay doubted it was possible to get out without the leaving being known. Still, he determined, he'd find out for himself come the first dark night.

The Rome brothers were planning a job. Of that, Clayton felt sure. Not wanting to be drawn into anything illegal, he tried to stay away from their camp. Yet he'd contributed his own small amount of money to the common pot, so it was the only place where he could eat.

Clay had felt that if he ate there, he had to do his share of chores. He had to admit he was the best cook of the four. The supplies were beginning to dwindle, so he wondered out loud while cleaning up at dusk one night if it would be possible to go up into the mountains and hunt meat.

"You must've ate loco weed," Jack exploded. "Ain't nobody ever goes up past the man's house."

Ty agreed. "Yeah, it ain't likely anybody'd let you, Clay. Why not come in with us on the job we got planned? We need a couple of good men to pull it off."

There it was, what Clayton knew was bound to happen. He still didn't know how he should answer the question. As he hesitated, Jack saved him from the need to answer.

"No, by God!" Jack Rome insisted loudly. "We need a professional, somebody that knows what he's doin'."

Ty got to his feet. He opened his mouth, ready to shout at his younger brother, but Orville stepped in. "Hold it, both of you."

Orville turned to Clay. "You see, we're divided on this. But since the subject's been brought up, you might as well know some more on it. It's about a day-and-a-half's ride from here. We could do it with four, but I, for one, would be a lot happier if there were five of us."

Jack growled from deep in his throat, but Clayton couldn't help voicing his thoughts. "I still don't know where or what you mean. But I'd never go on an expedition where Jack was involved. He'd shoot somebody, and in the eyes of the law, we'd all be guilty of murder."

The gunman leaped to his feet, his hard eyes blazing at Clayton. "There, you see? He ain't got what it takes to be in this business." Rome turned to his older brother. "Orville, you're almost as bad as Ty. Don't tell this greenhorn no more."

He stiffened his back and walked away.

Clay turned and looked at Orville. "Did you once say your plans have to be approved by the man?"

"Well, not everybody's do. But we don't have money enough to keep going till we pull this job off, so in order to get credit we got to have a plan the man likes. Then when we come back, the man gets a quarter of whatever the take is."

Clay saw a way out where he might spare hurt feelings. "Maybe you'd better wait for his word. He might want to send along somebody he trusts, just to look out for his own interests."

Orville heaved a sigh. "Yeah. What he said through Stoney was to get a better plan or more men."

Clay found himself interested even though he didn't want to be. He said, "Seems to me you ought to improve the plan rather than let more men in on the split. Especially since a full quarter is spoken for before you even leave here."

Ty spoke with excitement. "Show him the plan, Orville. Clay's good at figgerin' things out."

Orville looked from his brother to Clay. He moved over to a bare patch of ground, picked up a stick, and started drawing in the dust.

"For now, I won't name the town, but this line is the main street. Along this side, here, all the buildings are one story, and most have false fronts. Right in the middle of this straight stretch is the stage station. Across from it, at an angle, is the bank. Beside the bank is the hotel."

He paused to see that Clayton was following all he said, then continued. "Now, we know for a fact that a large shipment of money is coming in on the stage. It will have to be carried across the street to the bank. We want to be there when they cross with it, grab the money, and ride out of town to the east."

Orville stopped, and Clay wondered if that was all he was going to say. Clay glanced at Ty, then back at Orville, and asked, "Do you know for sure what day, or even what hour, the money will arrive on the stage?"

"Well, it comes to that town only once a month," Orville answered. "It will be the week closest to when the cattle drives finish. The ranchers around there all hold off paying their hands till they get back to town. So all we've got to do is have a man wait at the railroad's shipping point, then get a message to the rest of us."

Clayton shook his head. "Sounds like a lot of chances for a mistake. But just suppose it *does* work that way. How will you get the money away from the people who carry it across the street?" He didn't wait for a reply. "In fact, why not stop the stage outside of town a ways and not need to do the job right there in front of anybody who happens to be around?"

"Well. As to stopping the stage outside the town, there are two reasons. First, there's no good place where we could surprise them. Also, the fellow riding shotgun is a salty old bird, used to be a Texas Ranger. He's got a reputation for shooting first and talking later. But if we wait until the strongbox is off the stage, that shotgun will be in the station. I've watched him myself, Clay. He can't wait to make his report and get over to the saloon to wash the dust down."

He looked over to see Clayton watching him closely. "In the town, everybody will be relaxed, thinking they're home free. We can take them by surprise."

Orville had answered one question in great detail and ignored the other, Clay noticed. He let it pass and asked instead, "Which of these buildings is the office for the local law?"

Orville Rome pointed with his stick. "The town marshal and a deputy sheriff share the same office and jail right here beside the stage station."

"Then any resistance not already on the street will come from that pair of buildings," Clayton observed.

He looked from one brother to the other. It was obvious to him that the Romes hadn't seen past whatever guards would be on the street, nor how many guards might be covering the men who carried the money across to the bank.

Orville said, "The sheriff's deputy is out of town most of the time, since they've never had anything worse than Saturday night drunks to worry about. We'll just wait up at the curve of the street till they start across with the strongbox.

Then we'll ride down, knock the messengers and the town marshal on the head, and ride right out with the money."

Clayton squinted at the drawing in the dust. "What's on the curve up here at the west end?"

Orville's face went blank, but Ty Rome spoke up. "I looked that part of the town over. The building on the curve is a hardware store downstairs, and the second story ain't used anymore."

Clay thought for a second. "Is there a window that looks down on the street from the second floor?"

"Yeah, there is." Ty nodded promptly.

"You should have a man up there with a rifle, and one on the stage itself."

Both of the Rome boys stared at Clayton. Orville was finally the first to speak. "For a fellow who's honest and has never pulled a job, you certainly see all the angles."

Ty slapped Clay on the back and bellowed at his brother, "I told you he could sure figger things out. I bet the man'll approve this'n all right."

Next morning Clay walked away from camp, wanting to be alone so he could think. He hadn't slept well, because he'd kept turning over in his mind how he could pay his way while he looked for Merle Hollister. Clay realized he felt good that two of the Rome brothers wanted him in on the job they planned, even if he was determined not to get involved.

Without thinking, he headed south from his camp. Not wanting to meet anybody, he stayed west of the buildings that made up the town. He went toward the waterfall, which was the source of water for all of The Settlement. This put him closer to the man's house than he'd ever been before.

As he passed by, he glanced that way. Clayton made out in the shadows of the porch a big blond man sitting with a Winchester across his lap. Clay raised a hand in greeting. After a short pause the guard responded. Clay wondered what would happen if he went right up and asked permission to go hunting in the mountains, no matter what the Rome boys had said. If something didn't turn up in another day or two, he figured he'd have to try it.

Clayton reached the waterfall and sat in a shady recess against the cliff, where he could watch the sunlight on the falling water. He pondered his problem for only a short time before he saw Hank coming from The Settlement with a pair of pails.

Clay wondered which group had sent his friend for water. He waited until the boy set the buckets down, then stepped forward.

"Good morning, Hank."

The boy whirled around in surprise. "Huh! Oh, morning, Clay. You gave me a start. Weren't expectin' nobody up here."

"I saw you coming a ways back. Reckon I should've showed myself sooner."

"That's all right." Hank was pulling his shirt off. "I take a short swim when I come after water lots of days."

Clay grinned. "Sounds like a great idea. Mind if I join you?"

"Help yourself."

A thought struck Clayton. "Does anybody know you swim in this pool, Hank? Because if they do, they might object. I know for a fact that some of them get their water downstream from here."

"Naw," Hank answered easily. "Them as get their water downstream are the lazy ones, and they never see anything that ain't right in front of their noses."

He walked into the pool at the base of the waterfall. Clay soon had his clothes off and joined his friend. After the first shock, the cold water felt good. It had seemed to Clayton that every day he'd spent in The Settlement had grown hotter. He reflected on how badly he needed this bath, that he'd accumulated days of sweat and dust.

Clay looked up to see a rider on a tall, thin horse watching them. The man looked familiar. Then Clayton remembered the fellow was a friend of Grover's. He'd been the first to speak the day Clay had gone into the saloon looking for the gambler. The man just sat on his horse and watched with a silly grin on his face.

When he neither dismounted nor rode on, Clay asked, "What are you staring at? Haven't you ever seen anybody take a swimming bath?"

In answer the fellow merely laughed a soundless laugh and rode back toward the town.

After a time Clay and Hank got out of the water, dried, and dressed. Clay felt better than he had since Sid Ryder arrested him on that trumped-up murder charge

He said to Hank, "I'll walk back to town with you. Want me to carry one of those pails?"

"Naw, one in each hand balances me. One'd feel heavier'n two."

After that, Clay found a couple of buckets and helped his friend fill the water barrel in the saloon. As they neared the end of the dusty street on their third trip back from the stream, several well-spaced shots rang out. Clay observed, "Another day, another shooting competition."

"Yeah," Hank agreed. "I been hearing those so long, most of the time I don't even notice. You know, Clay, you might win some money in one of those games. Some of them fellers bet real heavy."

"But I might lose," Clayton answered, "and I've got nothing to bet."

"I got some money. I seen you shoot, and I wouldn't be afraid to bet it all on you."

Clay stopped. "Where'd you get money in this place? And, besides, Hank, just because I was lucky with Stoney and Beef doesn't mean I'd win. I could have a bad day and not be able to hit the side of a barn."

Hank just looked calmly into Clayton's face. "I saved money from what some of the fellers give me for running errands. It don't cost me nothin' to live here. I can always get a free meal at somebody's fire."

When they walked on, he turned at the saloon. "See you later, Clay. I got to carry some up to the man's house, and he don't like for nobody else to come along."

Clayton waved at Hank and went on. He thought maybe he'd just go and watch the shooting match for a while, see how good these fellows really were.

The games were held close to the outlet where the stream followed a rocky course out of the small valley. He stayed well back, waiting to see how the game was played and who was shooting against who. Clay watched several matches. When the competition was with a six-gun, Jack Rome always finished at or near the top. But later, when the targets were moved back and the weapon was a longer gun, the gambler Grover was the clear winner.

Clayton marked this fact to remember. Grover never wore a handgun out in the open. If he wanted to settle a score, he'd most likely try to do it at a long distance. Up close, he needed the surprise of a hidden gun.

Jack and some of the others who were interested only in the short gun matches had left when the Winchesters came out. One man who Clay had spoken to several times remained. His name was Davis. Although he'd not won either time, Davis had been a finalist with both guns.

When he noticed Clayton watching, Davis called to him. "Clay! Come and try your luck."

Clay came forward but declined. "Sorry. I'd like to, but I've got nothing to bet with."

"Well, then, let's shoot just for the fun of it. I got to find somebody I can beat."

Clayton grinned. "Better quit while you're ahead, Davis. You shoot against me, and you'll look a lot worse than you do now."

The good-natured bantering came to an abrupt end when Grover interrupted. "By God, you're a number one fourflusher. Tellin' Davis how good you are, then you ain't willing to take a chance on him beatin' you."

Clay turned slowly to face Grover. "At least I wear my weapons right out in the open. I don't need a hidden sleeve gun to take the other man by surprise."

The gambler still held his rifle. Clay figured Grover thought he wouldn't draw against him with a Winchester in hand. Grover's left hand slid forward along the barrel while the fingers of his right dropped to the lever action.

"Who in hell are you to tell me where or how to wear my gun?"

Grover's right hand jerked the lever of his rifle down. While it was coming back up, Clay shot him twice in the chest. The gambler's mind had sent out its message, and his muscles continued their work. But the force of Clayton's two slugs turned his body enough that the .45 caliber lead went past Clay and buried itself in the ground.

Clay watched the surprise on his opponent's face turn to pain. Grover's eyes went blank, and he fell in the dust. Clayton stood and watched as Grover's body made a couple of weak kicks. When he lay still, Clay holstered his gun and walked grimly away. This wasn't the first man he'd ever killed, but it still wasn't any easier to handle.

In midafternoon Hank found Clay sitting in the same recess by the waterfall where he'd been that very morning. The boy came up hesitantly.

"Clay. You all right?"

His friend answered with great effort. "Yeah. I'll get over it, but I never get used to it."

Hank looked at him. "Guess there ain't no way for you to know, but around here if you kill somebody, it's up to you to bury him. You get half of whatever he's got, like his hoss and any money in his pockets. That is, as long as he didn't owe nothing to the man."

Clay looked up. "What are you saying, Hank? That Grover's still lying down there in this heat, waiting to be planted?"

"Naw, me and Davis dug a hole and put the dirt over him. I brung you what he had on him."

Hank held out a wallet, the sleeve gun, a handful of coins, and a pocketknife.

"What do I do, divide this and take it to Mr. Wall?"

"Be better to take it all to him and let *him* split it."

Clayton got to his feet and walked out into the sunshine. Hank followed him, saying, "Davis went to saddle Grover's hoss. Stop at the corral down by the outlet, just west of where they hold the shootin' matches. Davis should have him ready by now."

"Thanks," Clay said.

Hank walked with him down the slope to town. Neither had much to say. When they passed through The Settlement, Hank went his own way to run some errands for one of the men. They parted with a wave.

When Clay got to the corral he found a big, good-looking geld tied to the fence and saddled with a fancy rig. Clayton looked around and saw Davis talking to the man who took care of the corral and its occupants. As he started in that direction, the hostler hurried away and Davis came to meet him.

Something clicked in Clayton's mind. He turned back to the black gelding and walked around it. There, on its hip, was a brand. A large letter *M* with wings. Sure enough, Clay thought, this was the horse that had been stolen from Walt McKenna at the Dry Creek Station.

Clay's brain whirled. Grover wasn't the gambler he was looking for, so how did he get this horse? Well, there simply had to be two gamblers, and if that was all there was to it, Clay had followed the wrong one. He'd probably lost the trail of Merle Hollister for good.

Damn! he swore silently, his jaws tight. Now, more than ever, The Settlement was a trap, a place where he could not stay honest and survive. Yet, he agonized, if he'd followed the wrong gambler, where had he lost Hollister's original trail and switched over to Grover's?

Into his thoughts, Davis came around the geld, slapped it on the shoulder, and said, "Some horse Grover had, ain't he?"

Clayton felt he had to be sure. "Davis, I know where this geld came from. I personally know the fellow he was stolen from."

Davis looked a question that Clayton didn't entirely understand. Clay asked, "Is there any way I can take this horse back where he came from?"

"Are you crazy?" Davis demanded. "Even if you got permission to take him out of here, the man who used to own him would most likely have you arrested. Or hang you himself."

Clay shook his head. "Not this fellow. Like I say, I know him. If I take his horse back, I'll have a friend over east of here where it might be important. I could go through there in a hurry someday and need a change of mounts."

This much, he thought, he'd explain to Stoney if he had to. What he wouldn't say was that he still hoped to find out for sure whether it was Merle Hollister, or Grover, who stole the black.

Davis took his hat off for a second to scratch at his dull brown hair. "Far as I know, somethin' like that has never been tried. I doubt Stoney would agree with you."

"I'm going to try," Clay answered, determined. "Thanks, anyway, Davis. Maybe someday I can repay you and Hank for all the two of you have done for me today."

He swung into the saddle and rode to the small house where he had talked to Stoney Wall the first day he was at The Settlement. Dropping the reins to groundtie the black, Clay stepped up and knocked on the door. He heard the floorboards creak as someone approached.

The door was wrenched open. Beef stood there, his manner curt. "Well?"

"I'd like to see Mr. Wall."

"If it's about you a-shootin' Grover, *I* can deal with that."

Clay thought to speak carefully and try to avoid negotiating with the bulky go-between. "There's more to it than that."

Suddenly from inside Stoney's voice ordered, "Let him come in. I'll talk to him."

Beef threw a hostile scowl at Clay, but he swung the door wide and moved back.

Clayton stepped into a room that looked out of place to him in such a rough town. The walls were of sawed boards fitted together well. A stone fireplace stood against the right wall, and a polished desk was at the left of the room. Stoney sat behind the desk and motioned Clay into a chair in front of it.

"So you settled with Grover. He was the gambler you were looking for when you came here?"

As he slid into the chair, Clay glanced at Beef, who had taken a stance to his right and slightly behind him.

"I'm not sure," Clayton lied. "But that wasn't why I shot him."

Wall appeared not to care about reasons. He said, "I guess your friends have told you that in a situation like this, half of whatever the dead fellow had goes to the man."

Clay handed over the wallet and other personal things Hank had given him. "I didn't go through his pockets myself, but here's all he had."

Stoney motioned to Beef, who stepped forward and went through the items on the desk. Stoney said to Clay, "You're lucky to have friends who'll help when you don't know how things are done."

He turned to his burly guard. "What horse was Grover's?"

Beef answered, "That big black geld with the Flying *M*

brand as come in here a week or ten days ago. Grover traded his own hoss and some stuff to boot for him."

"The way I see it, that horse is worth more than all these things together." Stoney's large hands swept Grover's fat wallet and other possessions into a pile. He looked to Clay. "A top mount is always worth more around here than money."

Clayton thought that if he was ever going to broach his idea, he had to do it now. He shot a swift glance at Beef.

Wall must have come close to reading his mind, for he said, "Beef doesn't like you, but it doesn't change a thing with me. For my own protection I do nothing he doesn't know about. So just say whatever is on your mind."

Clay decided to plunge in. "I happen to know that horse. I'd like to take him back where he came from."

Beef made a chopping motion with his left hand. Clay ignored him and hurried on with the story he'd rehearsed on the way up from the corral.

"The fellow who owned that geld has a niece. I'd stand good with both her and her uncle if I took him back. How could it hurt me to have friends where it could make a lot of difference if I have to change mounts fast?"

Wall had no trouble making a decision. "I'll go along with your plan. I'll take the money and other things here on the desk for the man's half. You take the horse and saddle."

He paused to give Clay a long look. "I understand you were the one to change the Rome boys' plan." Without waiting for an answer, Stoney continued. "The man was impressed. When you get back, I want to hear about that job as well as how you made out with the horse. You come and see me right away."

Clay stood up, careful to give nothing away. It might not do for Mr. Wall to know he had no intention of riding with the Romes.

Relieved that his interview was over, Clayton said, "Thank you. I should see you in a couple of days."

Beef stood still without saying a word as Clay passed him and walked out the door. He went on the lookout for Hank on his way through town, but even then, he almost missed his young friend. Hank was coming out of an alley. Clay swung the black over to meet him.

The teenage boy stared as he asked, "How did you get Stoney to give you the horse as your share?"

Clay grinned. "I'm not sure which argument convinced him. But I *do* know that if Beef had gotten his way, I'd have ended up with nothing."

Hank nodded as if to confirm how hard the big guard was to please.

"I'll be gone for a couple of days," Clay said.

Hank looked up quickly. "You goin' out on a job? Let me go, too. I could hold your horse, help with camp chores. I'd do 'most anything to get away from here."

Clayton wondered whether the kid wanted to get away for good or just for a spell, but he didn't ask. "Not this time, Hank. I'm only going to see a friend."

Clay hadn't realized how bad things must have been for Hank until he read the disappointment on his face. "Maybe we'll find a way soon," Clay said.

He left Hank standing, watching him as he rode away. Clay rode into the Romes' camp as Ty was starting the evening meal. He couldn't see Orville anywhere, but Jack, propped up against his saddle, appeared to be in a talkative mood.

"Take a hard look, Ty. This here feller what you and Orville like so good killed a man today. So look out. He likely reckons he's somethin' special."

Clay ignored Jack Rome's taunting. He asked Ty, "How long before we can eat? I'm riding out tonight, and I haven't eaten all day."

But Jack interrupted, hell-bent to make trouble. "Hey, hotshot. What'd you have to promise Stoney so's you could keep that good hoss of Grover's?"

Clayton refused to let Jack get his goat. He waited for Ty's answer about the meal.

"Shouldn't be too long, Clay. What little we got to cook don't take much to get ready. You go on and do whatever you need to. Orville should be along soon."

Up to now Clay had kept both his mounts staked close to camp. They had the grass grazed down for some distance around. He brought both the buckskin and the gray in and put his saddle on the buck with his bedroll and all his possessions tied on.

Jack watched him finish, then tried again. "Hey, mankiller. How about I take one of your mounts? You got three good'uns. That one I rode in on is mostly used up."

Finally Clay turned to answer. As he did, he saw Orville coming across from town. "Jack," he said, "you'd use up *any* horse you rode. You don't have sense enough to take care of the animal that takes you where you want to go."

Jack Rome was on his feet before Clay stopped talking. "I ain't Grover, and I ain't a-facin' you with no clumsy long gun. You never fronted a real man afore. The guns are loaded this time."

Clayton stood ready. He didn't want to kill another man, but he knew he would if Jack kept pushing.

"The choice of weapons was Grover's," Clay stated. "In one way you're like him, Jack. You just won't stop until you're dead."

Jack refused to respond. He settled into the crouch Clay had seen before, his hand like a claw over his holstered six-gun.

Orville shouted from several feet away, "Stop! Both of you."

His gunman brother's voice came out in a snarl. "Stay out of this. I'm a-goin' to make sure he don't interfere with our jobs no more."

Jack's eyes burned into Clay. "Draw, you bastard."

"You first," Clayton answered.

Ty moved to stop the action. He stepped in from Jack's right and to the rear, grabbed his younger brother's gun arm, and twisted it up in the middle of Jack's back.

"You damned fool, Clay would kill you."

Jack's mutterings were unintelligible as he struggled to free himself.

Ty looked at Orville, who was close now. "Take his gun till he cools off."

Orville lifted Jack's six-shooter and stepped back. When Ty released Jack, Orville flipped a silver dollar at him. "Go get a drink and settle down."

Jack Rome opened his mouth, shut it, and stomped off. His brothers and Clay ate their supper in silence. When he finished, Clayton got to his feet and said, "I'll be gone for two or three days. When I get back I'll find another place where Jack and I aren't always rubbing each other the wrong way."

Orville studied him. "The man approved our plan, with your improvements. I'd really like for you to come in with us."

"Yeah," Ty agreed quickly, bobbing his head.

Clay thought on how he could refuse. "Not this time," he finally answered. "Jack and I purely couldn't get along."

He paused, then felt he had to add in all honesty, "I doubt he and I will ever be able to work together."

Clayton mounted the buckskin and picked up the leads of the other two. Orville made to speak, but Clay rode away, directly to the corral at the beginning of the outlet. The hostler was just closing the gate as he rode up.

"I'd like to leave my gray with you while I'm gone."

The man turned and said, "Just run him into the big pasture. Be no charge if I don't have to do nothin'. If he needs takin' care of, I'll set the price. You think the bill's too high and can't pay, I keep the horse."

Clay watched the fellow while he made his little speech.

Something was familiar about him. Finally Clay blurted, "Seems to me I should know you."

"Yeah. I seen you in Agate a coupla times. Name's Sweeney."

When Clayton couldn't make the connection, the hostler continued. "Away from The Settlement I'm a horse trader. I sold Alf Billings this gray you aim to leave here."

Clay was momentarily off-stride from his shock. Then he thought, This fellow plays both sides against the middle. He shook his head.

"I shouldn't be gone more than three days," he explained calmly. "But my gray had better be here even if I'm gone a week."

Clayton, leading the black, turned the buck and rode down through the outlet. Stoney Wall must have passed the word, for the man on guard waved him on without a challenge. Clay had some trouble following the route he and the Romes had come in on, because it was just as black this night as then. But he worked it out and camped at the same stream where they'd all waited for dark on their way in.

Chapter Six

****

While Clay ate and rested for a couple of hours, thoughts of Mary Ward came to him. Disappointment that she'd not had faith in him flooded back. Funny, he realized, he hadn't thought about Mary the whole time he'd been at The Settlement.

Then Betsey McKenna came to mind for some reason Clayton didn't understand. But he knew her concern for him was something to consider. As he mulled over these things, he started out again. He rode through the day and got to Dry Creek Station just at dusk.

The same young, blond hostler was cleaning out stalls. Clay stuck his head in the barn door and yelled, "Hello, Blondy, are the McKennas home?"

"Yeah," the answer came, with no reaction on the bored face.

But Clay thought he heard resentment in the voice as Blondy continued. "The stage has been gone for over an hour, and they're both in there swillin' coffee. I s'pose you expect me to take care of your hoss. Ain't got enough to do, workin' day and night."

Blondy had really changed his tune since Clay came through here before, he thought. But all he said was, "I wouldn't dream of letting anybody else see to my horse. I want the job done right."

He left the black tied to the fence while he unsaddled the buckskin and rubbed it down, then turned it into a corral with other horses. Clay led the black geld to the front of the station, left it at the tie rail, and went inside. Walt McKenna sat with his back to the door, some papers spread out in front of him. Betsey was nowhere to be seen.

Clayton cleared his throat and said, "Mr. McKenna, I understand you know horses."

The stationmaster turned without getting up as Clay continued, "There's a horse out front here. Could you come look at him?"

McKenna stood and started toward the door. "Do I know you? Your voice sounds familiar, but I can't see your face good."

"I came through here one time before."

McKenna took a close look at Clay as he approached across the large room. "Oh, now I know you. You were looking for a gambler, the one who stole my horse."

Clay stepped back to the porch. He watched with pleasure the stationmaster's surprise, then glee, when he saw the big black geld.

"Glory be, you've brought back my horse!" McKenna turned, grabbed his hand, and began pumping it. "It's Clay, isn't it? Where'd you ever find him? You know, Clay, I've been worried about you ridin' west with the kind of people you did."

As McKenna was about to burst from his excitement, Betsey came out the door. "Clay! Oh, I'm so glad you're all right."

He stood and looked her over, content to let someone else be the first to speak. His silence didn't seem to bother Betsey at all, but her uncle spoke up.

"You'd best put another plate on the table. Clay has got to be hungry."

Betsey turned with a cheerful smile and hurried back through the main room to the kitchen. McKenna looked after her.

He said, "She sure is the best girl I ever knew. She's a

hard worker and really bright. One of these days somebody is bound to ride through here and claim her. And I sure would miss her."

The stationmaster turned back to his horse at the hitch rail. He stepped down to take a closer look.

"Where'd you get that saddle, Clay? It's sure not the one that disappeared off the corral fence when that gambler took him."

Clayton grinned. "It's the one that was on his back when I found him, so I guess it'll have to do in place of the one stolen from you."

Walt was running his hand down the horse's legs and picking up one foot at a time to examine all four feet. "He's been rode some, but I don't see any bruises. Doesn't seem to be any the worse for wear."

He walked around to the other side. "Boy, oh, boy! Will you look at that rifle?"

McKenna reached up and slid it out of the boot. "This is one of them new heavy-duty Winchesters, takes a forty-five/seventy-five cartridge. A salesman came through here, but what he wanted to sell me wasn't as fancy as this one. No, this long gun didn't come from the station. In fact, I didn't have a gun missing."

He stopped and looked at Clay. "If you give my horse back, you'll have nothin' to ride when you leave. What happened to the horses you had before?"

"My buckskin is out in your corral, eating your hay right now, and I still have my own saddle. If you didn't lose a rifle with the horse and saddle, I'd like to keep that fancy Winchester."

Clay looked at the stationmaster a minute before he added, "The fellow who had your horse was working the lever when I shot him."

McKenna looked Clay in the eye. Clayton met his gaze, unflinching. The stationmaster nodded and walked up the steps to the porch.

"I'll not be too curious about things, Clay. Just be careful what you say in front of that lazy Blondy. He's turnin' into a worse gossip than any woman I ever did see."

After the meal, Clay and Walt sat on the front porch talking quietly. Clayton told as much of what he'd been doing as he thought he dared. He still wasn't ready to lead the law into The Settlement, not until he found Merle Hollister and was cleared of murder.

"Walt, tell me something about the gambler who took your horse. Was he about five-five or -six, with a black coat and trousers that hadn't been cleaned in a long time? The man I took the black from also had an untrimmed beard."

"No, Clay. He was six feet, or close to it, with a well-trimmed beard. He *did* have a black coat and pants, along with a white shirt and string tie. But they were all clean and real damned neat for a man traveling around."

"That's the gambler I won the money from, and he could clear me of any charges against me," Clayton affirmed. "But I have to find him first."

McKenna remained quiet, and Clay got lost in thought. He pictured Merle Hollister sitting in the station's main room, winning at poker. Then, when everyone else was asleep, taking the black horse out of the corral.

Damn! Clay suddenly thought. The tracks that led west to The Settlement *must* have been his.

Walt McKenna cleared his throat. "Clay. There's more against you than you know. I've been reluctant to tell you, but I've got to now. When you broke out of jail in Agate, did you shoot the deputy? A fellow named Ryder?"

"No," Clayton said, startled. "He made me mad enough to want to, but I didn't. Besides, Sid Ryder was nowhere around when I got out."

Relief flooded the stationmaster's voice. "Good. I didn't think you had, and Betsey was absolutely sure you'd never kill a man the way it was told this Ryder died."

"Are you telling me the deputy was shot to death? And they think I did it?"

"Yes, Clay," Walt admitted softly. "I'm sorry to say, there's a flyer out with a fair likeness of you."

The weight of his words hit Clayton like a club. In a hoarse whisper he demanded, "Exactly what does it say on the wanted poster?"

"Just that you're wanted for murder in two separate incidents. But, Clay, you've got to be careful—it *does* say dead or alive."

The news held Clay speechless with shock for several minutes. Then his mind began to work. "Wait. It must have been Jack Rome, the one who rode in here last that day. He must have doubled back to Agate and killed Sid. But where did anybody get a likeness of me?"

He paused and remembered that there had been only one. Mary Ward had wanted to keep it, and he'd let her. Clay groaned loudly.

"Walt, it doesn't get any better. In fact, it couldn't get worse. They're going to make an outlaw of me no matter what I do."

Betsey stepped from the doorway onto the porch. "Clay, don't give up hope. I've been standing here, listening, and there simply must be a way to prove your innocence."

But Clayton barely heard her, his despair complete. He figured he shouldn't have been surprised that Mary had betrayed him, since she had openly thought he was guilty. Then his thoughts turned to Jack Rome. Clay knew he should have killed him back in camp. Or, better yet, left him in jail.

Betsey was speaking now, responding to something McKenna had said about going to bed. "Uncle Walt, I want to sit here and try to cheer Clay up a little before I come in."

The stationmaster got to his feet and reached a hand down to Clayton. "Betsey's right. Wait and see. Something could happen to clear you. In the meantime, for your own safety, I'd suggest you be well away from here before daylight.

Seems to be a passel of folks traveling the roads these days. It wouldn't be good for either of us if you were found here."

Clayton could feel rather than see Walt's kind, concerned eyes on him in the darkness. "Clay, you think on what I said the last time you were here. You could go a long distance away, grow a beard, change your name, and live a long life."

Clay stood up. "Thanks, Walt, but I don't think I can. Not any more than I could have when you suggested it before."

The stationmaster nodded ruefully, understanding, although he wished it could be different. He left Clay and Betsey to a comfortable quiet that stretched out between them. Finally Clay found himself talking, telling Betsey about himself.

Out came the revelation of his having been an orphan and of his knocking around the past few years. He could feel her listening, and the next thing he knew, he was telling her about his frustration with Mary Ward. He stopped abruptly, feeling awkward.

This time the silence was more anxious. Finally he blurted, "I hope you'll forgive me for burdening you with all my troubles."

Betsey spoke in her usual calm and practical tone. "That's all right, Clay. You needed to get it out so you can be rid of her now."

They talked awhile more on general topics. Then Betsey said, "I think I'll go to bed now. You should try to get some sleep, too. There are plenty of beds, with no overnight stage. Just take your pick."

She said good night and went in. But Clayton stayed on the porch and pondered Walt McKenna's suggestion that he should ride away and change his name. From there he again went over everything that had transpired. He still came to a blank when he tried to figure out what had happened to Merle Hollister.

It was a good time to think. An early moon lighted the

yard, but the big old cowhide-covered chair sat back in the shadows. Clay felt the need to hide now that there was a wanted poster out on him.

He looked carefully around the yard once more, then rested his head against the high back of the chair. The last thought he had was of Betsey telling him that now he had Mary out of his system.

When Clay woke, his head had slipped to one side. It felt like someone had tied a knot in the cord in his neck. He surveyed his surroundings, wondering what had gotten him awake. The moon was down, and he could see nothing.

After Clay sat awhile and rubbed his neck while listening to night sounds, he got up. As quietly as possible he took his buckskin from the corral and threw the saddle and saddle blanket over its back. Without attempting to tighten the cinch, he led the horse away.

When he was across Dry Creek, Clayton stopped and took care of the cinching. The buck gave its usual loud grunt, and Clay was glad he'd waited until he was away before mounting. Not having a second horse to spell the buck, his progress was much slower. Clay had plenty of time to ponder how he should handle Jack Rome.

In the end he decided that, as much as he wanted to confront the gunman, he'd do better to try to avoid a showdown. He couldn't know for sure, but it was more than likely that Jack was the only one who could clear him of killing Sid Ryder. He saw no way of getting Rome to do it but knew it would have to be done.

Clay awoke to the sound of falling water. For a minute he couldn't remember where he was, but then it came to him: he was by the waterfall just above The Settlement. He'd ridden in late at night. Recalling that he wanted to avoid Jack Rome at any cost, he'd come directly up here.

Clayton had arrived dead tired and had simply put a hobble on the buck and thrown down his bedroll. He couldn't recollect when he'd slept so soundly. Not when he camped with the Rome brothers, and certainly not on the way to Dry Creek Station and back.

Hell! he said angrily to himself. He was becoming an outlaw in mind if not in deed, if he could only sleep well here in this thieves' haven.

Clay pulled his boots on and set his hat at its accustomed angle on his head. He got to his feet and looked around carefully. Seeing nothing out of the ordinary, he walked over to the pool for a drink.

By the water's edge he saw tracks, made as recently as this morning. Clay took a closer look and recognized them as Hank's. The kid had to have seen him asleep there by the falls. It didn't really matter, since he totally trusted Hank. But if his friend could come that near without his hearing, then so could someone else.

Clayton drank. When the cold water hit his stomach he was reminded that his last meal had been night before last, the one Betsey McKenna had made him at Dry Creek Station. He thought on how he was going to eat again, with no supplies and no money.

What was it Hank had said? He tried to remember. Oh, yeah. That he should enter the shooting matches, since some of the men bet heavily. Clay had two Winchesters, his old saddle carbine, and the long gun that Grover had tried to kill him with. He thought he didn't need two rifles, and maybe he could sell one. This last one would bring a lot more than his older gun, but he was reluctant to risk it.

As he wondered what to do, he saw Hank coming up from the town. Clay waited for him. "Morning, Hank."

"Mornin', Clay. Did you have a successful trip?"

"I did what I wanted, but I'm still broke." His hunger forced Clayton to plunge right in. "Is there a shooting match this morning?"

Hank gave him a sharp look. "Yeah. But without either

Grover or Jack Rome to stir things up, it's sure quieter. Davis is a-winning more without them two.''

Clay stood up. ''Reckon I should mosey down that way and see if I can shoot straight enough to earn some eating money.''

Hank got excited immediately. ''I told you afore, I got some money. It's hid in a place that only I know about. Give me a half hour, Clay, and I'll lend you some or back your shooting. Or maybe both.''

The kid started away.

''Wait, Hank. Did you say without Jack Rome? Why isn't he shooting today?''

The boy turned back long enough to answer, ''The Romes and a coupla others rode out sometime in the night.''

Clayton nodded and swung into his saddle. Then he remembered that Stoney had directed him to give a report right away. Well, Hank's errand would take half an hour, so he thought he'd better see to this business first.

Clay dismounted in front of the house where Stoney held forth and knocked. Wall's voice called out, ''Come in if you're alone.''

Clay opened the door to find Stoney at his desk, his hand touching a six-gun on the desktop. ''Clay! Come in. Beef is out at the moment, but I *did* tell you to make a report as soon as you got back.''

He threw Clayton a hard look. ''I understand the Rome boys went out on that job without you.''

Unasked, Clay slid into the chair at the front of the desk. He felt more at ease without Beef watching and listening. Clay said, ''Jack Rome and I will never be able to work together. I'd kill him in under a week.''

Wall studied Clay a bit longer. He said, ''The man was unhappy that you weren't part of the job you planned. He was also not too pleased with the pair the Romes *did* take with them.''

Clayton said nothing around his mounting tension. Then

Stoney finally broke into what was almost a grin and added, "But that's nothing you have to worry about, Clay. Tell me about the good black geld. Did that work out the way you wanted it to?"

"Yes and no. Its owner and his niece are more my friends than ever. But they told me there's a dead or alive flyer out on me and didn't want me seen at their place. Can't say as I blame them."

Wall waved aside any extended explanation. "I want to know who and where these people are."

Clay stared at him and shook his head in refusal.

Stoney said, "I know they're your friends. You want to keep them to yourself and not subject them to having Settlement men stop there and get them in trouble with the law. But you're on this side now, Clay."

Here was one more thing pushing him in a direction he damned well didn't want to go. Clay got slowly to his feet as Stoney Wall's hand settled on the grip of the gun on his desk. Clayton felt cold, not like he'd ever felt before when he had killed.

Aloud he said to Stoney, "I'm not going to tell you. If that means you aim to use the desk iron, just remember there's a good chance I'll take you with me."

Their eyes locked, as two strong men were each determined to have their own way. Time stood still. After an eternity of moments, Stoney relaxed and let his hand slide away from the six-shooter.

"You're probably right," Wall admitted. "No purpose can be served if we're both dead."

His tone held no apology but was merely a string of practical words from a man doing what he had to do to stay alive. Clay held himself taut and ready, not sure if Stoney was playing a trick. He waited.

Stoney Wall gave him one more long, hard look before saying, "The man said your credit is good around town, starting now. Just tell anybody who challenges you that I said so."

"Thank you," Clay returned from between gritted teeth. He turned on his heel, left, and got his horse.

Mounting the buck, he reined it away before he broke out in a cold sweat. God, that was close! Clay realized. He'd never been that near to his own death before, and he was in no hurry to do it again.

Lost in thought, he let his horse go along with no guidance. When Clayton looked up he was near the Romes' camp, or at least near where it had been. Nothing personal of any kind had been left there, and he wondered if the three were coming back. But then, when he thought more on it, he knew they *would* be. They owed the man, and that was one debt even they would honor.

Clay rode the buckskin to the pasture and turned him in. His gray was there, in fair shape. Clay left his saddle with some others by the pasture fence and took all his weapons.

As he neared the shooting range he had two handguns in his belt and carried both the carbine and the fancy Winchester that had been Grover's. Hank was waiting and came to meet him.

"Be careful," the kid warned. "That big yellow-haired feller is one of the man's personal guards. I don't know what he's a-doing, shootin' with these others. Them as live up to the house on the hill don't come down here with us'uns lest something's in the works."

As Clay approached, the blond lieutenant was shooting. He made a series of long shots look easy, and that apparently finished the round, for at the end the other shooters paid him.

After he had collected his earnings, he turned to Clayton and said, "I'm Leon."

He didn't offer to shake hands, and like many others, he gave only one name. Without waiting, Leon continued, "Care to try your luck against me? Davis, here, is the only one that gave me any competition."

Clay thought, why not? He said, "That's what I came for. The only trouble is, I'm short on money just now."

Leon said casually, "Your credit's good with me."

He turned to Davis. "How about it? Want to try one more time?"

"Damned right." Davis grinned. "I got to get some of the money back that you just won from me."

Leon went on, as if used to being in charge. He looked at Clay and stated, "I see you came prepared for any distance. We'll make it a triple. First, for drawing and accuracy with the handgun. Then the middle distance with the carbine, and the real long distance with whatever rifle the shooter chooses."

He looked at the other two to see if they were agreeable. Clay nodded, and Davis said, "Yeah," then turned to Hank.

"Go get my Sharps," Davis ordered. "If I win, I'll give you some of it. If I lose, I'll be broke."

"But I want to stay here and bet," Hank protested. "I got some money."

The men looked dumbfounded. It was the first time any of them could remember the boy's being reluctant to run an errand. The only two not to show surprise were Clayton and Leon.

"Who you bettin' on, Boy?" Leon asked.

The answer shot right back. "Clay. To take both of you all three times."

For the first time, Leon grinned. "I'll cover whatever you got to bet, and we'll not start until you get back with Davis's big rifle."

Hank nodded and hurried off while the rest of the arrangements were put together. The three were drawing straws to see who would shoot first when the kid came back, carrying the big gun in both hands. Later, Clay wondered at his luck. Whatever he did at The Settlement had appeared to come out to his advantage, and now he was to shoot third.

It had been agreed that once a position was established, it

would hold all the way through. Davis was first. As he stepped up to start the match, Clay caught movement out of the corner of his eye and turned his head. Men were drifting over from the town. The word must have gotten out that something special was happening.

Five empty cans had been set up on a rock. Davis carefully aimed each shot and knocked them all off. Leon stepped up as the cans were replaced. His manner was more offhanded. Nevertheless, he leveled his gun at arm's length and knocked all the cans down.

As Clayton watched, he figured he'd best use his own method. When the five cans were set in place for the third time, he stood where he was, scooped his six-gun out of leather, and fanned it five times. The shots rang out in a single reverberating roar, and the five cans went off the back of the rock.

In the quiet after the shots Clay heard a comment from one of the spectators behind him. "Should've bet on that'un."

Another stranger said, "Damned show-off."

The first voice shot back, "Hell, you're just jealous. Ain't another man here could fan his iron that fast without sprayin' lead from here to breakfast."

A third chimed in, "Anyways, none of us could shoot that fast even if we wasn't trying to hit anything."

Meanwhile, the tiebreaking round was set up. It was almost a repeat of the stone-tossing test Wall and Beef had put Clayton through his first day there. Davis's shooting pleased the onlookers until he was eliminated when Leon hit four out of five stones.

When Clay's turn came, Beef suddenly stepped forward. "I'm throwin' this time."

As the stones were being selected, Leon looked at Clay with a question on his face. But it was Davis who spoke up.

"If we're goin' to be fair, we'd ought to have the same fellow throw for all three."

Beef locked Davis's eyes in a challenging glare. Clayton knew he had to be careful, since it was obvious the big guard hadn't butted in out of friendliness.

He fancied his performance as good as any traveling actor's when he heard himself say, "Doesn't matter to me. Either way."

Beef made a quick, clumsy move and launched the stones. Not only were they smaller than Clayton had shot at before, but they were spread farther apart. To make matters worse, the bald giant had not thrown them as high as the other man had for Davis and Leon.

Clay's timing was good. He got off four shots and shattered four stones at the top of their rise, in the split-second pause before they began to fall. The fifth had almost reached the ground when Clayton got his last shot off. The target disintegrated.

"The first round goes to Clay on draw and accuracy," Leon announced. No one wanted to dispute him.

The carbine competition ended in another three-way tie after shooting at stationary targets. Then somebody went and got a wagon wheel. Six tin cans were fastened to the spokes. Each shooter had up to twelve cartridges as the wheel was rolled slowly down a hill some forty yards away.

Davis went fast, firing all twelve shots and hitting three cans. The crowd was noisy in its approval. Leon hit three cans, too, but his style was more deliberate and it only took him ten shots to do it. The group was a bit more quiet and serious by way of congratulations.

Then arguments grumbled over whether or not that placed Leon ahead of Davis. But they went moot when Clay shot. The only question came down to whether he'd used ten or eleven shots to hit five of the moving cans.

"I could eat the rear end of a polecat," Davis said, breathing in amazement. "What say we take some time off and rest a little before the match with the long guns?"

He glanced from Clay to Leon and continued, "That's my best shootin'. I'd like to be ready for it."

Clayton looked to Leon and said, "I've been hungry for so long that I forgot what good chuck tastes like."

Leon laughed. "We'll take one hour and meet back here to finish this."

Hank stepped forward and walked back to town with Clay. "Where are we a-goin' to eat?" the kid asked.

"I've seen a place right in the middle of town. The man said my credit was good anyplace here."

Hank nodded, impressed.

They went to the eatery. Clayton was surprised at how clean it was. The food tasted good to him, but when Clay signed a credit paper the counter man insisted on, he saw that it cost a good three times what it would have back in Agate.

He and Hank ate in silence, the other customers leaving them strictly alone. Davis sat at a table in the far corner, but Leon was nowhere to be seen. Clay scooped his meal into his mouth and hurried the kid back to the shooting site.

When they got there, Clayton said, "I've never fired this gun I got from Grover. There's a good chance either Davis or Leon, or both, will beat me."

Hank looked at Clay and fought to keep a glum expression off his features. "Well, do the best you can," he managed to say. Then he grinned in spite of himself. "Bet you'll win, anyways."

"Tell you what," Clay said. "I've got plenty of loads for this rifle. Let's burn some powder and sight the gun in. I'll get used to it while the rest are feeding their faces."

Hank's grin widened. "How can I help?"

"Go to that rock shelf where they usually set up the long-range targets. I'll sight it in on that, then hold just under for shorter shots and higher for longer ones. You go out there and signal me after each shot, Hank. Tell me if I'm high or low, and how much."

The pair got so interested in what they were doing that when Clay finished and waved Hank in, he was surprised to see most of the spectators back from their meals. As he looked around, Davis stepped forward and spoke.

"Ready or not, Clay, we can't start yet. That Leon sure takes a long time at getting his belly full."

When he did show up, Leon made no apology or explanation but simply got down to business. "We'll shoot in our same rotation as before, starting at that rock shelf and moving the targets out until we have a clear winner."

They agreed and began the round. Shooting at the standard distance, Leon had a slight lead but not enough to be declared the best. The targets were moved back. It was close this time, but now Clay had the edge.

When the targets were moved another time, Davis began to shine. The targets were moved back a third time. At this longer distance Leon was soon eliminated. It became a struggle for Clay to stay even with the grinning Davis. They picked a target even farther away. Clay estimated the range to be close to six hundred yards.

He and Davis rode out to inspect the final target: a large rock that was a bit taller than a man and about as wide. They agreed that Leon would be the judge and measure who came the closest to the center of the rock.

Davis shot three times, and Leon marked the rock and signaled Clay to try his three. Clayton stepped up to the mark. He got down on his belly and used a forked stick he'd driven into the ground to rest the barrel of his rifle.

Somebody in the crowd yelled, "Now, that ain't fair."

Clay looked up at Davis. Davis shrugged. "Well, nothin' was said against it. I just never thought of it myself."

"When I'm done, you shoot again, the same way I'm doing," Clay said. "Then we'll count whichever is best."

Davis nodded his thanks, and Clayton waited for the onlookers to quiet. Then he settled himself, sighting on the center of the rock. He raised the gun until he was looking well over the top of the rock, held his breath, and fired.

Clay's rifle gave him an advantage. Davis was using a single shot and had to sight over from the beginning each time. While Clay's gun held twelve, he didn't have to reload each time like Davis did. When he finished, Davis tried again, but the rifle rest still worked better for Clay.

As Davis fired, a strong wind came up and blew across the range. When the whole group went to inspect the target, Leon pointed out that Davis's first three shots had been better than when he shot from the rifle rest. But Clay had all three shots in a close bunch near the top of the rock, while Davis had only one anywhere near the center.

Davis reached out a hand to Clayton. "Congratulations," he said with sincerity. "I'd never of thought anybody could beat me and my Sharps, but you done it."

Chapter Seven

****

Early the next day, Clay went to the pasture where his horses were kept. He spent a couple of hours working on his mounts: trimming hooves, combing, and currying. Hank found him there and wasted no words.

"Clay, you're wanted to Stoney's place right away."

Clayton had just finished with the four-year-old gray and turned him loose. "What does Mr. Wall want, Hank?"

"Don't rightly know, but they been a-having me tell fellers to come in all morning. I'm s'posed to have you and Davis come right off."

Clay nodded and went with the kid. On the way toward town Hank said, "Most likely they're a-picking men for some job. Leon's in the house with Stoney, but I ain't s'posed to know that."

"Thanks," Clayton acknowledged with a wave as Hank split off to look for Davis.

Here it was again, Clay thought. People and circumstances kept pushing him toward a life of crime. Damn, he wished he had a lead on Merle Hollister. How could he manage to stay around The Settlement and not go out on one of these jobs?

He hadn't found an answer by the time he got to Wall's house. Beef was sitting on the steps, but Clay made to go past him. The big guard stopped him.

"You're to wait and go in by pairs."

Clay turned, refusing to answer. He went to the same corner of the building where Beef had leaned that first day and watched him. Remembering the incident, Clayton rested against the corner in the shade and concentrated on a spot behind the guard's right ear.

Beef began to fidget after a while, then got reluctantly to his feet and turned to look at Clay. He shifted away, then turned back one more time.

"Damn you," he swore. "I know there's somethin' wrong about you. When I find out what, I'll break you up into little pieces."

Clayton grinned a deliberately unpleasant grin. "What's the matter, big man? Can't you take what you dish out to others?"

Beef's mouth dropped open, and a lame sputter fell out as he tried to find a way to get the best of Clay. He was saved by the arrival of Davis, gave up, and waved the pair in to see Stoney. Clay stepped up to the door, knocked, and entered without waiting. Davis was right behind.

Clayton glanced toward the desk and wondered where Leon was, since Hank had said he was there. Clay casually turned the other way and saw Leon sitting, relaxed, by the darkened fireplace.

The blond lieutenant spoke up immediately. "Clay, Davis. One or both of you might have guessed the real reason for yesterday's shootin' match was to find just the right men for a prime job. At least one of you'd ought to go. Actually, I'd like it if you both would. There'll be need of men with the kind of long range skills you both demonstrated."

Clayton struggled to keep a poker face, which was helped by the fact that Davis showed excitement.

Davis said, "The only reason Clay beat me was that wind blowin' when I shot the last time. I want to go whether he does or not."

"Good," Leon answered, "I like a man with confidence." He looked at Clay, who suddenly got a sinking feeling.

Clayton said the only thing he could think of. "I'd rather not this time. I came here to The Settlement looking for a certain man. You can call it single-mindedness or whatever you please, but I want to find him before I take on a job."

Leon waved a hand toward Stoney across the room. "I know somethin' was said about a gambler. Reckoned you'd found him when you killed Grover."

"No. He wasn't the one." Clay glanced at the man behind the desk and caught a quick breath. He said to Stoney, "You remember how your man Beef told us Grover had traded for that black geld? Well, I know the man I'm looking for rode that horse with the Flying *M* brand in here."

He paused for a minute, then continued. "He's a bigger man than Grover was, and better dressed."

Leon shot a quick glance at Stoney Wall. Clayton knew a message had passed between them, and that he'd have missed it if he hadn't been alert.

"What do you want this fellow for?" Leon questioned.

"It's personal, between him and me," Clay said without thinking. Then it hit him that the two knew something about Merle Hollister they weren't sharing. A tightness had formed around Leon's eyes, and his mouth looked grim.

Clayton added, "I don't have any grudge to settle. I'm not looking to kill him or do him harm."

Immediately, most of the tension that had built up in the room seemed to blow off. Stoney and Leon appeared to be waiting in case he would speak on.

"The gambler did me a favor once," Clay continued. "I need to see him about one further thing he could do to help me."

Leon nodded at Stoney, then turned aside to Davis and asked, "How good are you at followin' a map?"

Wall in turn said to Clayton, "You can go now, Clay. Maybe we can use you the next time."

Clay figured maybe he hadn't said too much, after all, even though he wasn't exactly sure what had just happened.

He was so glad to have it over with that he even smiled at Beef on his way out. The guard was obviously confused at his gesture, and Clay laughed out loud as he went around the corner.

Several days passed. Clayton felt more relaxed than at any time since he'd come to The Settlement. The Rome boys hadn't returned, and Hank insisted on giving Clay half of what he'd won in the bet over the shooting match. Clay could hardly believe how much the amount came to.

He had plenty of time to think now. As he mulled things over repeatedly, he finally concluded that Merle Hollister had to be one of the men who lived in the house on the hill. If not that, he must be so well known here that he could just trade mounts and keep going. Either way, Clay felt sure both Leon and Stoney knew more than they were about to tell him.

The problem was how to get information from one or the other. Clay wondered if it was possible to find out from Beef. He probably knew, too, but then he'd never tell the time of day if he could help it. If Clayton could only get a look at the men up there, he'd know for sure.

With Leon gone on the same job he'd recruited Davis for, there'd be one less lieutenant guarding the man. Maybe this was the time for Clay to do his night scouting up that way. He thought, if he was caught—well, hell! He'd either get away with it or be shot for a prowler.

When night came, he pulled off his boots and got the moccasins he'd taken from a brave he killed on the trail drive up from Texas. Clay headed in the general direction of the hill just after dark. He took his time, stopping to listen after every few steps.

The night was black. The only light came from the stars, since the moon would not be up until just before morning. Clayton followed the curve of the rock wall from the waterfall until he could see something ahead that looked darker than the rest of the night. He stopped again and listened for several minutes.

When he moved a few steps again, Clay smelled tobacco smoke and knew a guard was nearby. But how close, and exactly where was he? Almost no wind blew, but what small amount there was definitely came down the pass. So the fellow had to be in close to the house. A dim light came from one of the windows. The other way, along the side, was dark. Probably where the man's lieutenant was situated.

The side of the house was so close to the rock wall that Clay thought it impossible to pass the guard without being caught. So he drifted back away, then circled around the front of the house. After some time he came to the other front corner in the same careful manner. He could detect no presence.

Clayton stood still, waiting and listening. While he was unsure of what to do, the front door opened and a rectangle of light shined out. A man came from the house, and the door banged shut.

Clay felt trapped. If he moved fast enough to get out of the way, he'd be heard. If he stayed and the fellow was a change of guard, he'd run into Clay when he rounded the corner of the house. He heard footsteps coming and dropped to the ground, then rolled against the base log of the house.

Clay was barely in time. A heavy tread came around the corner. Just as a booted foot landed within inches of his head, a deep voice demanded, "Where are you, George?"

The answer came from nearby, and in a disgusted voice. "Right in front of you, ya damned fool. If you'd listen 'stead of blunderin' around in the dark, you could tell."

"Don't call *me* a damned fool," the angry answer snapped. "I've been takin' care of—"

A new voice from the porch cut through. "Shut up, both of you. What good are you if you can't keep your traps shut?"

After a moment George's voice spoke quietly. "Just afore

bigmouth here blundered around, I could feel something or somebody close by."

The fellow on the porch took command. "You go to the back corner, George. Barney, stay where you are. I'll get a torch. If somebody's around, the man will want to know."

Clayton was holding his breath. With his ear close to the ground he heard a swish of soft leather in the grass. He figured that had to be the one called George going to the back corner. Clay had to move before the one returned with the torch.

By turning his head, he could look up and see Barney against the night sky. Clay's only chance was to roll away from the building. If he could only get past Barney, he knew he could fade into the night and get away. With great care he rolled over once, then listened. Clay rolled again, and when he stopped, he heard Barney suck in a deep breath.

Clayton could feel him waiting. Damn! The other fellow would be back with the torch directly. He had to chance it; he rolled again. As he stopped he heard the whisper of metal against leather and knew that the fellow was drawing his gun. Turning his body slightly, Clay rolled once more as a shot split the night.

The time for caution was past. Clayton jumped to his feet and ran in a zigzag, bent double as he heard one, two, three .45 slugs whistle past him. He didn't worry about direction, as long as he got away. The sound of hot lead gave his feet wings.

Clayton's going took him slightly downhill. When it felt like his lungs would collapse for want of air, he finally stopped. The shooting had ceased, so Clay had time to think. What would those guards do now? he wondered. Would they let the episode go, or would they try to find out who'd been prowling around?

He immediately realized he couldn't take the chance and that he had to try to cover himself. Clay reckoned he could get young Hank to give him an alibi, but then he rejected the idea. Everybody knew they'd become fast friends and thus might not believe the boy. And anyhow, Clay thought, he'd rather not involve anybody else. Especially not a friend.

Clayton started to walk toward the lights of the saloon, not sure what he was going to do. As he went along the dusty street, he noted a large number of mounts tied at the rail in front of the watering hole. The volume of noise spilling out over the bat-wings was at least twice the usual. He figured some type of celebration was going on.

As Clay passed the horses he stopped and looked again. At least two were cayuses he remembered roping out of Alf Billings's corral in Agate the night he and the three Romes had broken out of jail. So the brothers were back in The Settlement, he concluded. That had to be what all the rowdiness was about.

Clay hesitated a second, then walked along the side of the saloon building and slipped into the back door. He entered a pitch-black storeroom and had to feel his way along to the sliver of light coming under the door to the barroom. When he reached it he eased the door open a crack. Nobody was looking his way. He inched into the saloon and closed the door.

Right in front of him stood the end of the bar. Lying on the floor there, half-concealed from the room, was a man who'd already succumbed to whatever he was drinking. Clay reached down and got the fellow under the arms, dragging him to the rear door and propping him up there. He stepped to the bar, picked up the beer glass the fellow had emptied before collapsing, and signaled the bartender for a refill.

The man with the apron scooped up the empty, filled it with a dark brown liquid, and sat it down in front of Clay. Then, reaching under the bar, he produced a bottle of rotgut and added a healthy slug.

In a hoarse, gravelly voice the bartender said, "I don't know how you stay on your feet, as much of that as you've put down."

The man didn't expect an answer. He was gone to tend for another customer before Clayton could reply. Clay lifted the mug and took a cautious swallow. He almost gagged but managed to get it down. He had stood at a variety of bars in the past few years but had never tasted anything as bad as this. Glancing around to make sure he wasn't a focus of attention, Clay slid along the bar until he got to a spittoon. He poured half the drink into it and resumed his position at the end of the bar.

Now that he had time to survey the other patrons, he saw several he knew, at least by sight. At the center of the celebration stood Jack and Ty Rome, so he reckoned their robbery must have been successful. Jack was buying drinks for the whole group. Ty just stood there, already three sheets to the wind.

Clay started looking around for Orville. Just as he sighted Orville sitting at a table with another man, the bat-wings burst open and three fellows walked in. Without knowing how or why he knew, Clayton was sure the one in the lead was the man who had gone after a torch when Clay had almost gotten caught at the house on the hill.

Behind him was a youngish fellow, wearing a pair of tied-down guns that looked well taken care of. Clay somehow knew this one, too; he was the man called George. The third was Beef.

The first man stopped just far enough from the bat-wings to make sure he wasn't outlined to anyone outside. George took several steps to his right. Beef moved to the left until he stood at the far end of the bar from Clay.

At a signal from the fellow in the center, Beef banged on the bar with the butt of his handgun and bellowed, "QUIET!"

When he had everyone's attention, the first man said, "We're looking for a prowler. If he's here, he would have come in within the last half hour."

He paused while most of the drinkers looked around at

one another, then continued, "Any of you knows anybody that just got here, I want you to tell me."

He looked to the barman. "Has anybody just come in, Mart?"

The aproned fellow glanced around helplessly, then shrugged. "Ain't seen nobody, but then I been real busy."

Clay tried to hear all that was said without being obvious. He swung his gaze from the fellow in the middle to Beef and found the big man looking at him with malice plain on his face. To cover his shock, he lifted his mug and drank. The stuff burned all the way down and kept burning long after it hit his stomach. Beef was still studying him when he put the mug down.

Clayton started to return the stare but remembered he was supposed to be drunk. He let his head hang down as if looking into what was left of his drink. Clay thought that, from his position at the end of the bar, he had as much command of the room as the other three did. If worst came to worst, he could do a lot of damage with two handguns. But he *did* wish he hadn't cut off his own escape route by propping the drunk against the back door.

He looked up cautiously. The one in charge glanced at George, to his right. The young gunman shook his head. The boss then turned to Beef, who gave no signal that Clayton could see. Then Beef turned his head back to look at Clay and started toward him along the bar. The drinkers who had been leaning there backed away to let the big guard through.

In the seconds it took Beef to reach him, Clay considered drawing his guns and commencing to shoot. But he knew there was no way he'd come out on top. Every iron in the room would be against him, and there were too many.

He slouched against the bar and let his whole body sag. Keeping a blank look on his face, he watched Beef come toward him. The guard stopped and merely glowered.

Clay looked back vacantly for several seconds. Then he

said in a slurred voice, "Hello, big man, why'n't you join the fun? Good ole Jack there would be happy to buy."

Beef hovered there and scowled. When Clayton felt too tense about it, he raised his mug again and finished the dark liquid. Then he turned to the barman. "Fill 'er up."

Mart came along and reached for the empty. Beef leaned over and stayed his hand, never taking his eyes off Clayton. "This hotshot ain't really drunk. When did he come in?"

"He's gotta be," the barkeep protested. "All that stuff he's downed. Fact is, I don't see how he can still be standing up."

Mart looked from Beef to the fellow who had come in first. The fellow said, "He sure looks drunk to me, Beef."

The bald guard wasn't satisfied. "I know this'n. You'd oughtn't trust him."

He shot a look behind Clay and said, "He could of come in the back door. With Mart so busy, he could've missed him."

Clayton was hard put to keep his foolish grin in place. But then a new voice spoke up, and it was George's. "That there door only opens inward. Ain't nobody got in through it with that drunk a-layin' right up agin it."

Clay glanced up with quick caution to see several heads nodding in agreement. But Beef said hotly, "Well, I don't know how he worked it, but he's the one as done it. I know he did."

With that he turned and went back the length of the bar and out the bat-wings. The leader nodded at Mart and said to the room at large, "Go back to your celebrating." He, too, left.

Clay stood there trying to look inebriated rather than deeply relieved. He could still feel somebody scrutinizing him. Continuing to play drunk, he looked up into the iciest pair of blue eyes he'd seen in some while. The young gunman hadn't left with the other two.

George smiled, but his voice held a challenge. "They tell

me you're the fastest man with a gun that has ever hit The Settlement."

He dropped his smile and pitched his tone for Clayton's ears only. "When you're sober I'll expect you to prove it."

He left the saloon. Clay glanced around the room. Most of the men had gone back to their drinks, some to gambling games. Clay leaned on the bar a bit longer, wondering how to get out of the place without attracting any more attention. When he looked up again, Orville was walking across toward him. Orville Rome wasted no words.

"Clay, you're entitled to a share of the money we got on that job. The whole thing worked like greased lightning. That is, until Jack overreacted to a hand motion and shot a man who didn't even have a gun."

Clay flinched, then looked at Orville and wondered if he needed to keep up his act. Orville didn't wait for Clayton to speak.

"Ty and I talked it over on the way back. You earned a full share of this one, and we both want you with us from now on."

"I could never work with Jack." Clay wondered how many times he'd said it before.

Orville nodded slowly and said, "Let's get out of this noise. I've got the take, and I'll get you your share."

He took Clay by the arm and started for the bat-wings.

Later that night Clayton moved his camp clear across the valley to an outcropping of rock by the horse pasture. The next day Hank asked what was going on.

Clay said, "I want to be close to my horses and away from the falling water. That constant sound not only might mask someone's coming up on me, but it dulls my senses."

Hank nodded. "Somebody like Jack Rome. Right?"

"Yes, him and others, too. I doubt many here would face me in an even break, with all that's happened. That doesn't include the fellow from up at the man's house. The one called George."

A perplexed look came over Hank's face, so Clayton told him all that had happened the night before. To finish his story, Clay pulled a wad of paper out of his pocket.

"Did you ever see any of these greenbacks before, Hank? They're supposed to be just as good as gold or silver coin. It's sure a lot lighter to carry around."

The look on Hank's face turned almost comical as he demanded, "Where'd you get that?"

"Orville Rome gave it to me. He said it was my share of the take from that job they just did. Said my plans made the difference, and I should have a full share."

Clay hesitated a moment, considering exactly what he wanted to say. He was aware of Hank's attention riveted on the pile of paper in his hand. Clay spoke, hoping that saying the words out loud would clear up his own thoughts.

"I just don't know. I need money to survive here, maybe more than any other place. But the trouble is, this is stolen money. Can I spend it and not think about the people it was taken from?"

Hank stared at him. "Hell, Clay, you got to eat! Is this here any different from what money we won at the shootin' match? After all, that was stolen from other people, too. Well, you was willin' to use that. I don't see no difference."

Clay shook his head at his young friend's practicality. He couldn't disagree. "I guess you're right. I'm already an outlaw, like it or not. The worst thing I ever did was to break jail when they were fixing to hang me for a murder I had nothing to do with. Now there's a flyer out with my likeness on it. It offers a reward, dead or alive."

"Clay. Let's me and you ride out," Hank blurted suddenly. "We'll not come back, just keep on a-going far away to where ain't nobody ever heard of either one of us."

Clayton shook his head again, slowly. "Not this time, Hank. I might have to, someday. But when I leave this part of the country, I want to do it with my name cleared.'' He grinned at the kid. ''It's almost noon. Let's go put on the feed bag.''

Hank agreed, and they went to eat. They were just finishing their meal when Orville and Ty Rome came in, looked around, then came to their table.

''Mind if we use that other pair of chairs?'' Ty asked as he and his brother pulled out the wooden seats and dropped into them.

''Doesn't appear to matter what we think,'' Clay said around a big smile. ''You're both already sitting.''

Orville gave an order to the man behind the counter, then looked at Clay. ''The truth is,'' he said quietly, ''we want to go out on another job right away. Oh, I know it'd be better to lay low for a while, but we picked up this information by chance the last time out. Both Ty and I want to take advantage of it.''

Clay stared the older Rome straight in the eyes and asked, ''What about your other brother? Is he part of this?''

''Jack? No. When he found out I gave you a share, he almost went out of his head. I thought for a while he was going to draw on me. But he let me off when he found out I gave you the paper money. He hadn't even wanted to bring it along, thinks it's worthless. He just picked up his bedroll and left. Ty and I won't include Jack in any jobs we do from now on.''

Clayton looked from Orville to Ty for a long minute. Then, with a rush, he decided to tell them how he felt. ''I think you both know I haven't done anything against the law. Except for breaking out of jail in Agate. I only want to clear my name and get away from here.''

Orville nodded and made to speak, but Ty's words came out first. ''But, hell, Clay, you got a knack for knowin' how a job had ought to be done! Me and Orville don't know how to make it any other way, only by takin' what we need from others.''

Worried and excited at the same time, Ty Rome's tone sounded short and choppy as he continued. "You got everything a fellow needs, Clay. A fast draw. You shoot straight, and you're smart. Hell, we could be in clover with you to lead us."

"And sooner or later we'd end up in jail," Clayton snapped back. "I didn't enjoy those hours in Agate. I don't ever want to go back."

Ty tried to retort, but Orville held up a hand to silence his brother. "Clay, will you tell us what you think of our plans? Just to help out a couple of friends? You don't have to go out with us."

Young Hank had been listening intently. "Clay," he put in. "If we got us a stake, we could get away from here whenever we wanted. Ain't no way you could be sent to jail if you never went out on a job."

Here it was again, Clay realized. Everything, everyone he knew was pushing him. He looked over at his friend.

"Hank, I know how badly you want to get out of here. Believe me, I want that, too. But is it any less dishonest to make plans for a job than to go out and take the money at gunpoint?"

The kid's head hung down. He said to his dinner plate, "My pa was honest and hardworking, and he's dead." He paused a moment before adding, "Leastways if you stayed here and helped with the plans, you wouldn't be a-shooting folks like him."

While Hank pleaded his case, Orville sketched on the back of an envelope with a pencil stub. "You see, Clay," he said, "here's our problem. There's a shipment of gold bars coming over the old Cherokee Trail. Ty and I, and now you and Hank, are the only ones who know about it. It doesn't belong to some lucky prospector; this is a big shipment that belongs to a company. It won't be guarded by soldiers. This company has hired its own guards. They thought men in uniform would tip off that the shipment was special. They're trying to look like a group of travelers going back East.''

Before Clayton could answer, Ty burst out, ''Dammit all, Clay! Just help us get the thing organized at this end and neither me nor Orville will ask you again. You don't have to do no ridin', and we won't shoot nobody who ain't a-shootin' at us.''

Orville turned his sketch so Clay could see it. ''Here's how it looks to Ty and me. That old trail runs mostly south, but somewhat north of the state line it swings east for a ways, then south again.'' He pointed. ''Right along here there's a blind canyon where we figure to camp and wait for the shipment. There'll be wagons in this group. When they go by, half our men can ride over this high pass. It's rough going, but good saddle stock can make it. They would be out ahead of the gold bar shipment.''

Orville Rome's finger stabbed the crude map. ''Right here the trail runs through a narrow place with rock walls too high to climb. That's where we'll wait and stop the wagons. Ty and the other half of our men will be behind them.''

He stopped to glance at Clay before continuing. ''They'll be boxed where they can't get away, and we'll end up with enough gold that none of us will have to ride out on a job again.''

Clay sat rubbing the back of his neck. He spoke slowly at first, but his words flowed faster as his own plan unfolded. ''Yes, you'd likely get whatever gold there was, Orville, but you'd have to kill all the people with the wagons. And some of your men would get killed for sure.''

He rubbed his neck again. ''Could the people with the gold bars be made to think that this blind canyon was the trail, until it was too late?''

Orville considered, then said, ''No. There'd surely be more than one guard that had been over the trail before.''

''Right,'' Clay had to agree. ''No, that wouldn't work.''

Hank looked from one to the other, then quietly got up

with a satisfied grin on his long, skinny face. He walked away as excitement built up in Clayton's voice.

"A better way would be to separate the guards from the wagons. Orville, you should camp here where you said but ride out in a bunch and hit the wagons from the front. Then, when the guards get involved in the fight, just ride for the canyon. The guards will follow you in."

He stopped to think for a brief second. "Have some men there to block the entrance so they can't get out, while the rest ride over the high pass. Leave a man or two at the top with rifles, and you'll have most of the guards cut away from the wagons, boxed in until you're ready to let them out. The main group would have easy pickings, with only the drivers to protect the gold."

Clayton arched an eyebrow. "Of course, I'm gambling that the wagons would keep right on down the trail when the guards rode after you. The next question is, how many men are you going to need?"

Not expecting an immediate answer, he quickly went on, "As I see it, the number depends on how many wagons are in this train."

"Reckon it'd be more important to figger the number of guards than the wagon count," Ty said.

"No. It wouldn't matter about the number of guards, once they're separated from the wagons and decoyed into the blind canyon. A couple of men at each end could pin them down."

"What do you figure, Clay?" Orville asked. "Two men per wagon?"

"Yes, that would do if they're the right kind."

Orville looked to Ty. "You ride out and see if you can find out how many wagons there are going to be. I'll try to get Clay to help me pick the men to go with us."

Ty Rome's expression held doubt. "That clerk what told us about this was shot up real bad. He only told us 'cause he thought he was dying and he wanted to get even with somebody. I never did figger out who."

"If he was only a clerk, he might not know, anyhow," Clayton said. "It'd probably just be a waste of time. Can we find out any other way?"

His gaze went from Ty to his brother, and finally Orville spoke. "I don't see any other way. Gold bars aren't that bulky; I'm sure they'd all go into one wagon."

He stopped, and Clay waited. After a minute Orville continued, "Of course, the load *would* be heavy if they're trying to make folks think they're merely travelers going back East. They'd need to spread it out to, say, three wagons, and mayhaps a couple more to look good. Say five wagons, ten men plus those left at the canyon to hold the guards."

Clayton considered and reconsidered everything that had been said as he got up to leave, and on through the day. The following morning he started to sort out the men Ty Rome sent to him. Meanwhile Orville presented the plan for Stoney to relay to the man for approval.

Sundown of the second day came just after Clay had chosen his twelfth man, and Orville brought the consent of Stoney Wall's boss. The man had also furnished the location of ranches where mounts could be left for quick changes on the way back after the holdup.

Chapter Eight

****

A new day began, and with it the Rome brothers started explaining their plan to the men Clayton had picked. Clay sat watching quietly until he felt sure there was nothing more he could do, then got up to leave.

Orville broke off from the rest and called to him. "We leave shortly after midnight. You'll be here for your share when we get back, won't you?"

Clay stopped to face the outlaw who had become his friend. "I'll be here till I'm satisfied the man I'm looking for *isn't* here." He spread his hands out. "After that I won't promise anything."

"Hang around and wait for us even if you find him," Orville urged. "You know you'll want to hear how it went, and your share should be a real chunk of cash."

A new thought came to Clay, and he voiced it. "Orville, how do you aim to turn those gold bars into money you can spend?"

Rome answered without batting an eye. "The man will take our share off our hands and give us money we can spend anywhere."

Clay nodded, thinking the man would make a big profit there, too. "If I'm not around when you get back, hold my share until I come for it."

"You bet I will." Orville Rome put out a hand to shake, and Clay returned the favor.

Then Clayton walked away to find Hank and see if the kid

wanted to ride with him to the Dry Creek Station. He told himself he needed to talk with Walt McKenna, but he had to admit he was really going to see Betsey.

It was his first time out of The Settlement, yet Hank rode calmly beside Clay from the time they mounted just at dark until they made camp well past midnight. Clayton had offered the kid his gray but had gotten a surprise.

"No, thanks," Hank had said. "The blaze-faced bay is mine, I just ain't never rode him."

Then, seeing the question on Clay's face, he continued, "Fellow named Porky gave him to me. Said if'n he didn't get back off his last job in two weeks, he'd be dead and I was to have the bay."

But Sweeney, the horse trader who took care of the herd, had been of a different opinion when he saw Clay and the kid leading the bay out of the pasture.

"Just where the hell do you two think you're goin' with that hoss?" His stance was belligerent.

Hank bristled. "Sweeney, you know damned well that Porky give him to me."

The horse trader had shifted his feet to make sure he could see both Clay and Hank. "No, kid, I don't know nothing of the kind. Rules say, any mount left behind belongs to the one takin' care of him."

Clayton had watched a red wave creep up the back of Hank's neck; it was the first time he'd seen his young friend angry.

Hank had answered Sweeney through clenched teeth. "What you said's only true if'n you done work to take care of him. And if'n ain't nobody else claims him. Besides, Porky *did* give me this bay. If you don't believe me, just you ask Davis. Davis was right there when Porky said so."

Sweeney had sneered. "It's real convenient for you that Davis ain't here. So I say you can't take that hoss. Leon and

Davis ought to be back in another day or two. You'll wait until then."

Clay knew it was time for him to take a hand. "Tell you what, Sweeney. Let Hank take the bay. When Davis comes, if he won't back Hank up, I'll stand good for the price."

"No, that won't do. How do I know as you got that there price? I got no way of telling that the both of you ain't equivocating."

Clayton handed the lead of his buck to Hank and stepped to the right. In a quiet voice he challenged Sweeney, "You want to spell that out? Are you calling me a liar?"

Some of the color had drained from the hostler's face as Clay spoke on. "Because if you are, either you take it back or go for your gun."

Sweeney had hesitated. Clay said, "Make up your mind. Whichever way is all right with me."

Clay's reputation at The Settlement and his calm confidence had seemed to convince the trader. But in an attempt at saving face, Sweeney had answered, "Well. So long as you're leavin' your own gray for security."

"No," Clayton countered. "I'll not leave him for security. You take my word, or else call me a liar."

The horse trader had seemed to wilt, but Clay didn't miss the gleam in his eyes as Sweeney went on. "I got me a contract to sell Alf Billings six top mounts. Without the bay, I'm short one."

"That's not my worry," Clay had retorted, his tone hard. "My gray had better be here when I come back, or this place will need a new wrangler."

Sweeney glared, then nodded and turned away.

"Do I make myself clear?"

The hostler had refused to face Clay. He merely nodded again and moved off.

* * *

When Clay and Hank had settled down for what was left of the night, Hank asked, "You think Sweeney'll try to sell your gray in place of my bay?"

"No, for two reasons. First, he knows what I'll do if I don't find the horse there when I go back. And second, Alf Billings, who he's selling those six mounts to, would recognize my gray."

With that Clay turned over and went to sleep. When he woke again it was morning. He and Hank mounted and rode into Dry Creek Station, arriving late in the day. They found Walt McKenna cleaning stalls.

After greetings and introductions were made, the stationmaster announced, "That damned Blondy must have gone and gotten himself thrown in jail again. He went to Agate night before last and hasn't come back yet."

"Did you say *again*?" Clay interrupted.

"Yes, he did the same thing once before. I went looking for him, only to find that the new deputy had tossed him in the jug. He'd been drunk and causing some kind of trouble. Guess I should've asked more questions, but I was in a hurry. Just vouched for him and brought him back. If I could find any other hostler, I'd leave Blondy in jail."

McKenna stretched and let out a groan. "I got another hour's work here, even if I hurry, Clay. Why don't you go on up to the front and see Betsey?"

Clayton grinned. "If you have another fork, I'll give you a hand, and it won't take only half that long."

Walt shot him an odd look. But before he could answer, Hank said, "Find *two* more pitchforks and it'll go faster still."

McKenna found them, and the work got finished. As they entered the waiting room of the station, Betsey came out of the kitchen.

"Who have you brought with you, Uncle?"

A sudden smile lit her angular face. "Clay! How wonderful to see you! But is it safe for you to be here?"

He grasped both of her hands and all but fell into the

depths of her hazel eyes. "I don't know, Betsey. But I have to get away from that place every so often, just to keep track of who I am. There's a whole valley over to The Settlement, but I still get some kind of a cabin fever. Then, too, if I'm honest, I just plain wanted to see you."

If Betsey had been prone to blush, the awareness of another pair of eyes on her forced her to remain composed.

Clay turned a bit. "Betsey McKenna, meet Hank. He's been the kid brother I never had."

She graciously reached out a hand. Then after a minute she said, "Supper will be ready in half an hour. All of you smell like the stable. You, too, Uncle. Why don't you go and get cleaned up?"

Laughing, they went out to do as she asked. After they ate, Hank helped Betsey with the dishes while McKenna and Clay went to the front porch to smoke and talk. When Walt had his pipe loaded and drawing well, he spoke through a cloud of smoke.

"You'll mark I didn't say anything about Blondy in front of my niece, Clay. But there's something more to his going to town than just to get drunk. I can't exactly put my finger on what it is, but I know in my bones that Blondy's not all up-and-up. At first I thought it might have something to do with you."

"Oh?" Clayton arched an eyebrow. "How so?"

"Well, he left right after you were here the other time. Then he went again the other day, and there wasn't any way he could've known you were coming. So now I don't know what to think."

After a short pause Clay asked, "What made you think Blondy's going to Agate and drinking too much had anything to do with me?"

McKenna took so long to answer that Clay was about to give up. Then the older man said, "There again, it's more of a feeling than anything else. But he did ask for the day off that same morning after you were here before. At the time I thought nothing of it, but later, when I went to Agate, I began to wonder. Both him and that new deputy said he'd been drunk, but the son of a gun sure didn't look hung over to me. And when we mounted up to head back here, the deputy came out and told Blondy to keep in touch."

Clay was still sorting through all McKenna had told him when the stationmaster continued. "Mayhaps I'm slow to catch on. I still never put any of these things together until the other day, when Blondy was getting ready to go to Agate again. He started to talk about you, Clay. Never put it in the form of a question, but he sure as hell wanted to find out all he could about you."

Clayton sat looking at the sun as it went down behind the mountains. He wondered if he could ever stop watching his back trail.

Walt spoke again. "Both Betsey and I think you're right, and the law has made a big mistake. But we can't risk any trouble with them, so I'm asking you again this time to be gone when the sun comes up."

As he got up to leave, his hand dropped onto Clay's shoulder. "I know how hard it is for you, and I wish I could help more. But the truth is, I'm already worried about Betsey. If you hadn't had this hard luck, I'd be all in favor of what I see happening between you and her. But . . ."

His voice trailed off, and Clay thought to help him out. "I understand, Walt. There's one thing I'd like to ask."

"Whatever I can do without hurting the girl, I'll sure do."

Clayton spoke in a low tone. "It's the boy, Hank. If I can talk him into staying, would you take him in? The Settlement is no place for a kid his age. I've tried to be a big brother, but the things I have to do just to stay alive there don't set a good example for him. If he doesn't get out, he'll go bad. I hope it's not too late already."

"You just betcha," Walt agreed without stopping to think about it. "He can take the place of the son I never had."

"Thanks. That really takes a load off my mind. Of course, you'll want to keep him away from strangers for some time."

McKenna gave Clay a long look, then said, "Right," and walked away.

It was as if Betsey had been standing in the shadows, waiting for her uncle to leave before she came out on the porch to see Clayton.

"Your friend Hank was a big help," she began. "Then he asked if he could go to the stable and turn in."

Clay could see enough even in the twilight to tell that Betsey wore a wide grin. She continued, "I convinced him it would be fine for him to sleep in the large bunkroom here in the station."

"Then Hank's asleep already?"

"I'm sure he must be." Betsey paused, then asked, "Clay, is it just the long ride that made Hank act so worn out?"

"Well, he only slept three hours last night. But he's used to taking care of himself."

"The way you've taken care of yourself?"

Her question was so sudden and sharp that Clayton wondered exactly what she meant. He studied Betsey's face as he said, "Hank's almost like a brother. I want him to have more of a home than I've ever had. Your uncle said he'd be welcome here, if I can convince him to stay."

"Yes, I'm sure Uncle has settled it. He'll stay and help run the station." She stopped long enough to breathe out a big sigh. "I wish you could stay, too, Clay."

When he opened his mouth to respond, Betsey laid a finger against his lips. "Shh. Let me finish. I eavesdropped shamelessly while you and my uncle were talking. I know that Walt is right, but I want to give you something of myself."

She urged him out of his chair and onto an old, broad, hide-covered bench, sliding down beside him. "Tonight is for you to have and to remember. Not to hold you or bind you in any way."

* * *

Clay came awake with a jolt and wondered what had alerted him. The sound repeated, from down at the stable. He tried to shift away without disturbing Betsey, but she stirred and yawned. Clay gently pulled her head close to him and whispered in her ear.

"Slip into the house without making any noise. Wake Walt and Hank. I think somebody's trying to steal the horses."

Betsey nodded and moved inside with the silence of a shadow. Clay slid his feet over the side of the bench and came up to a sitting position, feeling around on the floor for his boots, hat, and gun belt. Leaving his rifle where it rested against the back wall of the porch, he slipped quietly down the steps.

Clayton wished he had the moccasins he kept in his saddlebag. The yard was made of gravel from the creek bed, and he couldn't move without hearing it crunch underfoot as he walked toward the horse corral. Halfway, he stopped to listen. He strained his ears but could hear nothing and had to wonder if whoever was with the horses had already heard him.

After what felt like a long time, a voice said, "Must be a false alarm. Get that gate shut. You two take the back door, and I'll go in the front."

Clay heard the gate bump against the post as the speaker continued, "I want him alive if possible. But don't get yourselves shot."

A different voice, one Clay knew he'd heard before, spoke up. "Like I already told you, we'd best shoot first. I seen him draw and fire. If you give him a chance, some of us'll be dead. Maybe all three."

When a third person chimed in, Clayton recognized immediately that it was Blondy, the hostler. "The reward is dead or alive, ain't it? So I say, go in with guns out and burn him down as soon as you see which one is him."

Clay suddenly knew that he was marked to be captured or killed by these three. When the second man spoke again, he remembered where he'd heard the voice before. At the horse pasture for The Settlement.

That damned Sweeney! Clay told himself. But how did he come to be with Blondy? He reckoned the other fellow had to be the new deputy from Agate, the one they'd gotten to take Sid Ryder's place.

"For my share, I'll be satisfied with that pair of horses in the corral," Sweeney was saying.

Clayton was dimly aware of the words. He was considering that he couldn't let them go into the station with guns blazing, that he had to protect Betsey and her uncle. Not to mention Hank. He could hear two of them going toward the back door and the other coming directly for him.

Clay backed silently to the wall of the way station and waited in the shadows. As the deputy passed close to the corner of the building, Clay drew his gun and stepped up just behind the man. He brought his iron around in an arc intended to take the new lawman out of action for a little while. But the deputy heard him and started to turn.

In the short time it took for Clay's gun to come around, he heard the whisper of metal against leather and knew the deputy was in the act of drawing. As the man swung around to face Clayton, the blow that had been aimed to land behind his right ear nicked him high on the forehead instead.

The deputy's gun had just cleared leather, and his finger jerked the trigger. Clay had no idea where the bullet landed, but the fellow crumpled to the ground without a noise.

Clay turned to face the opposite direction, where he was sure the other two must be by now. He was just in time to see the flash as one of them shot toward him. Clay fired as he heard a .45 slug bury itself in the wall of the station building.

The sound of someone running toward the stable was soon drowned out by Blondy's voice swearing in pain. Before Clay could level a shot at the fleeing Sweeney, the front door banged open.

Betsey called out, "Clay! Are you all right?"

He moved in her direction, answering quietly. "I'm fine. I think Blondy's been hit, and that new deputy's taking a little nap. I hope he comes to with nothing worse than a headache."

As Clayton started up the steps, Betsey came down. She stopped one stair above him, flinging her arms around his middle and burying her head into the hollow between his neck and shoulder.

"Thank God," she said, sobbing.

His response was to hold her tightly in his arms, as Walt McKenna came through the door with a lantern in one hand and a six-gun in the other.

"Betsey!—Clay, are you all right? Did they get away with any of my horses?"

Clay released Betsey and answered the stationmaster. "They weren't after horses, they were after me."

Walt stood still in the quiet dark. After a short pause he lifted the lantern high and looked at the pair. Clayton continued, "Fellow I think to be Agate's new deputy is out cold over by the corner, there. Blondy's around by the back door, probably bleeding some. The other one got away."

Walt shook his head, surveying the area.

"Clay, this is too much," McKenna burst out. "I like you fine, but you can't keep on coming around anymore. Just get away safe, we'll take care of things. But no matter what my niece says, you can't be seen here again."

Stung by the raw truth, Clay turned and walked blindly down the porch steps and toward the corral. He kept his head down, damning his bad luck, when he heard Hank's voice yelling from the direction of the stable.

"Oh, no, you don't! I told—" The rest was blasted away by a gunshot, followed by the sound of wood splintering.

A horse squealed as if in pain. The drumming of hooves faded away in the direction of the dried-out creek bed. The ensuing silence deafened Clay. He realized that Hank must have gotten out in all the confusion and made it to the corral, only to confront Sweeney there. The horse wrangler must have shot at the kid as he tried to keep the bastard from leaving.

"Hank! Oh, my God!" Clayton shouted out loud as he started off running in that direction.

He came pounding to the corral to find his young friend holding up a broken gate by way of keeping the horses in the enclosure.

"You all right, Hank?"

The kid's voice came out sounding furious clear through. "Yeah, but that no-good Sweeney got away from me."

Clay couldn't see Hank well and thought to make sure. "He was shooting at you. You're not hit anywhere?"

"Onliest thing I hit was the ground, hard enough to get the wind knocked out of me, when I tried to shut this here gate in front of Sweeney. He was a-tryin' to steal your buck and my bay."

"But you're sure he didn't get any lead into you?"

"Naw. Sweeney couldn't hit the broad side of a barn in daylight, much less in the dark."

Clay realized he could see the kid now. McKenna had come up with his lantern. Walt must have heard enough to gather what had happened, for he said, "Here, Hank, you hold this light. Clay and me can patch the gate enough to hold till daybreak."

Hank took the lantern. While they worked, Clayton asked, "What about the deputy, Walt? Are you going to be in trouble because I knocked him on the head?"

"Don't worry about him, Clay, he's still out. Me and Betsey put him on that big bench on the front porch. She's keeping watch of him and will let us know in time for you to get away without he sees you."

"Before I go," Clay said, "I want to check on Hank one more time. And if Blondy's able to talk, I want to know how he and the other two got together."

Walt thought a bit, then asked, "Has Blondy or the deputy seen you and Hank?"

"Neither one saw me, but they knew I was here. Or at least they came with the idea of collecting the bounty that's on me," Clay answered. "I heard Blondy say to draw guns and shoot me down as soon as they saw me."

Hank spoke up. "That hoss trader Sweeney knew me, but I never seen the others."

Clay turned to the kid and questioned, "How did you get down here to the stable without running into one or the other?"

"I went out the window after Miss Betsey said somebody was trying to get hosses out of the corral. I heard a ruckus in the yard and come through the window to make sure they didn't get *our* mounts."

Clayton looked back toward McKenna. "Hank will have to ride with me this time. It would be too much of a coincidence if he stayed around here now."

They finished the gate in silence and started back to the station. Hank followed, carrying the lantern. He looked from one to the other, trying to fathom what they were talking about.

"Right. Next time," McKenna agreed. "Clay, I'll take Blondy into the kitchen. You stay outside and listen. I'll get everything I can out of him. Damned yellow belly, trying to collect the reward on a fellow he hasn't got the guts to face!"

Clay said, "Find out how he and the deputy and that horse trader happened to team up. I already know Sweeney doesn't like me and that he wanted Hank's and my horses."

"Right," Walt concurred again. "Here, Hank, give me that light, and I'll go on ahead."

Clay and Hank waited while Walt went to the back of the house and found his hostler. "Well, Blondy, here you are." He spoke loudly to make sure of being overheard.

The pair in the shadows couldn't make out the younger man's reply.

McKenna began again. "What in hell did you bring down on me?" He held his lantern high.

Blondy sat with his back against the rear wall of the station building, his right hand holding onto his bloody left shoulder. His face looked white in the light of the lantern.

"Me?" he demanded. "I didn't bring nothing on you. It's that damned outlaw as keeps comin' here to see your hoity-toity niece."

Walt McKenna put on a good show of blustering. "Outlaw! You mean the young man who comes courting Betsey? He's no outlaw, and my niece is certainly not hoity-toity."

Blondy's voice came to Clay and Hank loud and clear now. "She puts on airs. Wouldn't take a second look at an honest fellow, but she'd rather sit out on the porch with somebody wanted by the law."

The stationmaster opened his mouth, but Blondy cut him off. "He *is* wanted, even if you don't know it. I seen his picture on a wanted poster in the jail office more'n once."

Walt must have felt he was getting nowhere with this line and so pretended to notice for the first time that his hostler was injured.

"Why, Blondy, you're bleeding! Here, let me help you up. Now, put your good arm across my shoulder, and we'll get you into the kitchen."

As the pair went around toward the back door, Clay heard Walt say with concern in his voice, "When we get inside, you sit in that big chair by the window. I'll see to your wound."

After they disappeared through the door Clay could hear no more conversation. He and Hank sneaked up and stood on either side of the open window. McKenna already had Blondy's shirt off and must have been cleaning the wound, for the next sound they heard was Blondy's swearing and moaning.

Walt was all sympathy. "I know it hurts like hell, but we've got to get it clean."

There was a pause, then he continued. "There, that bandage will hold. Blondy, I'm sorry I came down on you before I knew you were shot. But how in hell did you and the law get mixed up with that horse trader?"

"I went to town on purpose to see the deputy, 'cause I knowed that Clay feller was the same one on the poster. If I could collect the reward, it'd make me a good stake. But wasn't much me and the deputy could do, so we went to have a drink."

Blondy paused to get a breath. "While we was there we got in a poker game with this hoss trader and that Billings feller as runs the livery. One of us must've mentioned something about this here outlaw and wantin' to collect the money on him. So this Sweeney speaks up and says he can tell us where to find him. We talked on it some and decided to come and see if he was tellin' us straight. We tried to get Billings to come, too, but he said as how he never thought Clay was guilty. So we came without him."

Clayton heard a door open. Then Betsey's voice said, "Uncle, the deputy has been conscious for a while and wants to get up. I talked him out of it, but I can't hold him much longer."

Walt must have figured he'd gotten all he could out of Blondy because of his answer. "Right, honey, I'll come with you. Blondy'll be all right here until I want to talk to him again."

Clay and Hank went quietly toward the corral. They had their horses out and the makeshift gate closed by the time Betsey came, carrying the rifle Clay had left on the porch.

"You'll need this," she announced matter-of-factly.

Clayton looked up from saddling. "Thank you, Betsey."

He hesitated, needing to say more but not sure how to say what was on his mind. Then he blurted, "I want to see you, Betsey, but your uncle is right. As long as I'm wanted by the law, I put you in danger every time I show up."

Betsey's tone was low and sure. "I want to be with you,

Clay. And Uncle said only not to be seen. If you want to talk, come after dark. My window is the last one on the far side of the station."

She waited. After a tense minute he nodded. Betsey almost smiled, then turned and walked away. Hank was already mounted and moving out. Clay was torn, wanting to stay and knowing he couldn't. He watched Betsey blend with the shadows, then swung into the saddle and followed Hank into the night.

Chapter Nine

****

Clay and Hank had to camp, waiting through most of the afternoon hours. It was accepted by all the outlaws as necessary to arrive at The Settlement well after dark. Still, the pair arrived only minutes after Sweeney, as was proven when they saw his lathered and lame horse. But search as he would, Clay couldn't find the wrangler.

He finally gave it up for the night, and in the morning he went to check with Stoney Wall as was expected of him. Clayton knocked at the door. When he got no response he tried it and found it fastened from the inside. He walked around back and found a rear door.

As he stood wondering if he dared try that one as well, he caught movement out of the corner of his eye. Clay looked up quickly toward the big house where the outlaw boss lived. Beef was heading toward him, waving for him to wait. Clay couldn't help but wonder what the big bald man might want from him. Then he figured Beef was more likely just trying to deliver a message from someone higher up.

"You're to wait," Beef ordered when he got close enough. "Stoney will be along directly."

Clay said, "Good. That's who I'm looking for."

The guard gave a leering grin, then answered in a gloating voice. "You won't think it's so good when Stoney hears what Sweeney has to say."

He started away toward the shacks and cabins that passed for a town. "Wait," Clay called after him.

Beef turned back. "Say whatever you got to say, and be quick. I still got to find the kid and get him here."

"Good," Clay said again. "I was just about to suggest you get Hank, anyhow. He was a witness to the things Sweeney's complaining about."

A new thought came to him, and he asked, "Is Davis back from that job he went out on with Leon?"

"Yeah. They're back, rode in just afore dawn the same night you and the kid rode out."

Clayton grinned widely. "Then ask Davis to come along, too."

Beef stood and looked Clay over, then shrugged and went on his way. Clay didn't have long to wait until he saw Stoney and Leon coming from the house on the hill. He found himself wondering where Sweeney was, and if the trader had told some trumped-up story calculated to get Clay into trouble.

Stoney invited them all in, and they went. Leon said, "We'd best wait to talk until the kid gets here."

Wall nodded and added that Sweeney should be along, too. Then it was Leon's turn to nod. The big blond man studied Clay as if trying to read something in him, and Clayton could only wonder if he was satisfied with what he saw.

Clay wasn't sure whether his wait was long or short. He didn't know enough about what was afoot to speculate on what might happen, so he turned his mind in another direction. A thought of Betsey McKenna came immediately to him. He looked up to see both Stoney and Leon still watching him, realizing that his daydream must have put a smile on his face. The smile broadened into a grin.

Leon commented, "This fellow enjoys waiting, Stoney. He must like the kind of thing that makes most men nervous."

Stoney nodded and made to speak, but the front door banged open. Beef pushed Hank into the room, followed a moment later by Sweeney. Clay glanced over to see uncertainty on the hostler's face, soon covered by a bravado of false confidence.

But it was Stoney who took prompt control. "There you are, Sweeney. I want you to repeat your story in front of Clay and the kid."

Sweeney licked his lips before he started to speak. "This here pair stole a right good blaze-faced bay out of the pasture and took him over yonder to that Dry Creek Station."

Clay was bout to refute the statement when Hank burst out, "That's a damned lie!"

The boy meant to go on, but Sweeney commenced talking right over what Hank was saying. "Then, when I went there trying to get my hoss back, they sicked the law onto me. I had to ride for my life, and on a lame hoss, to boot. Barely got away. I doubt if I'll ever be able to trade mounts across the line in the States again."

He stopped to catch a breath. Once again Hank made ready to speak, but Clay stepped forward and rested his left hand on his friend's shoulder.

"Let's make sure the horse trader is done first." He turned and gazed intently into Sweeney's eyes. The older man tried to give as he got but couldn't hold against Clayton's stare.

"Damn you," the wrangler muttered. "I could of handled the kid if you hadn't butted in."

Clay held his look hard against Sweeney, then spoke in a quiet voice that held the attention of everyone in the room. "So you came running here to see if Stoney or Leon, or maybe even Beef, would fight your battles for you."

The statement hung in tense air. Clay's eyes held a promise that made Sweeney sweat as Clay turned to Beef. "Did you ask Davis to come as I requested?"

The burly guard wasn't intimidated, as Sweeney had been. "No, I didn't. He ain't got nothin' to do with what's goin' on here."

Clayton glowered at Beef and let the stress build between

them. Stoney appeared willing to let it go on until one of them broke, but Leon spoke up.

"What has Davis got to do with this?"

Although the question was for Clay, Hank jumped in to answer. "Davis would tell that Porky give the bay to me. So I wasn't a-stealing him."

Leon shot a look at Stoney, and Stoney turned to Beef. "Go get Davis."

The guard stomped out. Wall said to Clay, "Normally I wouldn't listen to a complaint from one man against another. Like I told you that first day, you settle your own troubles. And it usually turns out like it did between you and Grover. That's good for The Settlement; it weeds out the slow and the weak. But Sweeney, here, is a special case. He keeps us supplied with the best horseflesh, which is a must in our business."

Clay considered this for a moment. Did it mean he couldn't get fair treatment? Not feeling sure, he thought he'd better play it safe. He took a quick glance around the room. With Stoney Wall in his usual place behind the desk and Leon across by the fireplace, they were one on each side of him. When Beef came back, all he'd have to do was stop just inside the door and Clay'd be caught in the center of a triangle.

Clayton let his smile die and his face take on a worried expression. He began to pace back and forth across the length of the room. On the third pass he stopped just inside the doorway, looking like he was deep in thought. He heard the creaking of the front steps and moved to the right corner of the room. This put him behind the door, with both Stoney and Leon facing him.

Neither missed the significance. A sardonic smile came to Leon's face, while a troubled look crossed Stoney's. But neither had time to comment before the door swung open and Beef barged in. He stopped when he couldn't immediately see Clay.

"Where . . . ?" He turned to find Clayton almost behind

him. As he looked to first Leon and then Wall for explanation, Davis slipped in and slid along the wall to the left of the door.

It looked like a Mexican standoff. Not even young Hank missed the meaning of where each stood in relation to the others. Davis grinned and opened his mouth to speak before the placement of people in the room dawned on him. Then his mouth went shut with an audible snap.

Clay thought it time for him to take control. "Davis, tell all of us," he directed, "did a man named Porky give a blaze-faced bay to Hank?"

"Sure did," Davis responded. "He—"

The rest was interrupted by Sweeney, who had been standing in the center of the room with Hank. He grabbed the kid from behind, his left arm around Hank's throat in a strangle-hold and his six-gun in the boy's ear.

"Don't anybody move, or he's dead. If I get away, you'll find him by the last guard on the way out. Anybody makes a wrong move, and this iron goes off."

Sweeney backed past Beef to the door and started across the narrow porch. Clay went quickly to the door where he could watch. If he got a chance, he meant to take it. Sweeney must have heard him move. He turned to look back just as he got to the top of the pair of steps.

Hank felt the twist of his captor's body. He let both knees buckle under him, and his weight against Sweeney's arm pulled him loose from the man's grasp. He rolled down the steps while the horse wrangler went headlong to the gravel at the bottom.

Clay's gun leaped out of leather and into his hand, but he found himself unable to shoot even a man like Sweeney in the back. Sweeney never looked to the porch where Clay stood. He scrambled to his feet and began to run.

Clayton jumped to the ground and took after the trader, determined to make him turn around. Sweeney swung both his arms with the motion of his body, trying to gain more speed, and Clay could see that he didn't hold his six-gun. He wondered if Sweeney had dropped it back into the holster out of habit or if the fellow had some plan to try to get the best of him.

They ran down the street between the few buildings that made up The Settlement, heading toward the horse corral. When Sweeney got to the last cabin on the right, he went around the corner in a crouch. Clayton had to wonder whether he'd stumbled or had dived, intending to make a stand.

He didn't have to wait long. Sweeney's gun muzzle came around the corner at just above ground level, spouting flame. Clay felt the tug of lead as it cut through his rolled-up sleeve, just above the elbow. He dived into a roll, thinking that if Sweeney had taken but a second more to aim, Clay would be down and bleeding in the dust.

He stopped his roll. Lying on his stomach, he threw a shot at the corner. Wood on the edge of the building splintered, and Sweeney swore. Then Clay could hear him running again. He jumped to his feet and continued the chase. When he rounded the corner the horse trader was running full-out again.

Clay knew Sweeney must have felt sure he wouldn't shoot with his back exposed. Clayton shouted, "Stop and face me like a man, you bastard."

The words acted like a whip to the running hostler, but Sweeney's riding boots were made for the saddle and not for running. A stone rolled under his right foot. The speed he'd built up betrayed him, and he lost his balance. It took him three clumsy steps to fall.

He came up with his weapon in hand again and managed to get off the first shot. Clay had no idea as to where the hostler's lead went. He skidded to a halt and shot Sweeney. The horse trader's body jerked, and he tried to level his gun. Clay took his time and put a .45 slug into Sweeney's heart.

Clayton walked slowly back the way he had come. As he did, he reloaded his gun, just to be sure. When he got to

Stoney Wall's house, Hank was sitting on the bottom step and holding both hands to his throat, with blood visible on the side of his head.

Stoney, Beef, and Leon were standing in a row above the kid. Leon nodded silently. Beef's face held a new look as he acknowledged Clay. Could it possibly have been respect? Clayton wondered.

"He's dead?" Wall asked tersely.

This time Clay nodded.

Stoney said, "Get him underground and bring his personal things up. We'll treat it like any other shooting."

He turned and entered the house behind Leon.

Clay ignored Beef and went to Hank. "Are you hurt bad?"

The kid merely shook his head, so Clay asked, "Did he break your Adam's apple?"

Hank tried to answer but only got out a croak that sounded like, "Don't think so."

"Can you swallow?"

Hank tried. Clay could see that it hurt, but he also noticed his friend could manage. He said, "Next thing is to clean up that skinned place on the side of your head. Then it'd most likely be good if you'd lie down for a while."

He helped Hank to his feet. The boy's limp was more pronounced than ever, but he could move under his own power. As soon as Clayton had Hank's head cleaned and bandaged, he tackled the job of burying Sweeney.

Davis offered his help, and Clay accepted. Then, while they were digging the grave, he asked so many questions that Clay began to wonder whether he'd helped out of friendship or curiosity.

When the job was done Clay gathered what he could find of the dead man's possessions and took them to Stoney. He dumped them on the desk without stopping to inspect what he'd brought. When Stoney went through the pile, he came up with a pair of bank books that showed the horse trader had large amounts of money in two different banks, plus a well-filled wallet.

Stoney Wall pushed the wallet across to Clay. "Here, you take this. What's in these two accounts is several times the amount you have there."

"Can you get that money, since he's dead?" Clay asked.

A slow smile crawled across Stoney's face. "I think we can. We have the account numbers, and there's a man here who can duplicate anyone's signature."

Clayton nodded and went to leave, but Stoney's voice stopped him. "I'll expect you to take care of the horse pasture for a while, until we can find another trader."

His eyes held Clay's for a spell as if waiting for a challenge or an objection. When he got neither, he turned away in an obvious dismissal.

Hank slept the rest of the day. Clay reflected that his young friend must have been tired out from the trip, that the business with Sweeney shouldn't have been that hard on him. But then, they hadn't slept much the two previous nights, and, too, Hank was *used* to plenty of sleep to balance all his hard work.

It wasn't until the following day that they had a chance to sit and talk. They were at the horse pasture. When Hank asked about his chief concern, the subject somehow surprised Clay.

"What did you mean about my staying with Mr. McKenna?" the boy demanded. "And that I couldn't stay right now, because it'd be too much of a coincidence?"

Clay looked at Hank and knew the best answer was the truth. "I wanted to talk you into staying and living at the way station. I guess coincidence wasn't the right word after all, Hank. You see, I was concerned that McKenna's hostler, Blondy, and that new lawman might somehow put things together and connect you with The Settlement."

The kid sat awhile looking at Clay, then asked, "Does that mean you don't want me ridin' with you?"

"I think of you as the younger brother I never had," Clay said slowly and deliberately. "There's no telling how long it will take for me to clear my name. This Settlement is no place for you to finish growing up. At least I wouldn't have to worry about you if you were with Walt and Betsey."

Hank said no more, but Clay couldn't tell for sure what he was thinking.

Toward sundown Clayton stopped at the saloon, in a rare mood for a drink. Gloom had already settled into the place, but Clay could see the bartender well enough.

"Let me have a shot of your best whiskey," he said.

As his eyes adjusted to the rest of the room, he could see that it was nearly full. But not caring as to who might be there, Clay turned back to lean on the mahogany and sip his drink. He felt rather than heard someone come up behind him.

"So, hotshot. I hear you killed another man," Jack Rome's voice announced. "And here all the time I was thinkin' you wasn't for real."

Clay studied the little gunman, trying to find a way to avoid what he felt was coming. Jack must have mistaken the silence for weakness, because he turned around as if to grandstand before the crowd. In the pause before Rome opened his mouth, Clay was aware that someone had come in the door and stopped to listen.

Jack Rome spoke. "I hope all of you recognize Clay, here. He's a real big-time killer. The last fellow he done in was somebody we all knew, old Sweeney that used to make sure we had the best hosses when we went out on a job. You know, old Sweeney, as had trouble getting his iron out of leather at all. Well, speedy, here, done him in. Don't rightly know, but I reckon Clay'll make sure we got some old plow hosses to ride from now on."

Clayton could feel his control slipping. He wanted to plant his fist in the middle of Jack's face. Jack turned his back on the rest of the room, obviously knowing most of the men were with him, and faced Clay.

"Yeah. Sweeney's a real notch on your gun. Ain't another man here that couldn't of given him a head start and killed him with his gun still in leather."

Too much, Clay thought hotly. No self-respecting man could take this and not defend himself. "Jack," he growled, "one of these days you're going to push too far, and I'll give you a dose of what Grover and Sweeney got."

Rome sneered, almost laughing outright. Then, speaking so low that only Clay could hear, he said, "You can't take a chance and try to outdraw me. Even if you got lucky and my iron hung up, you couldn't kill me. I'm the only one who can clear you of the murder of that deputy sheriff."

He paused to indulge in a malicious grin. Clay knew at once that there would never be a way to get Jack to vouch for him. Fleetingly, he wondered how brothers could be so different.

Jack talked on. "Sure. You and I know I'm the one what went back and done for that fool lawdog. But you got the credit for it with the local sheriff, and by this time he's passed it on to others of the law."

Clay's mind raced back to the night in question. The only time Jack could have killed Sid Ryder was while Clayton was riding toward the Dry Creek Station with Jack's brothers, he reasoned. That meant Orville and Ty could alibi him! It dawned on Clay like a great flash of lightning that he *didn't* need Jack Rome, that he never had.

Jack didn't see Clay's right hand move, but suddenly there was a .45 pressed against his chin. Clay's voice was calm and cold.

"Now, then. If you think you can outdraw me, Jack, I'll just return this to the holster and give you the head start you were talking about."

Rome's eyes riveted on Clayton's finger, curved around the trigger. Neither moved for a slow eternity of seconds. Then Clay took a half step backward and dropped his six-gun into leather.

"Now we can start even," he said. "You go whenever you're ready." After several seconds he continued, "What's the matter, Jack? You were always so sure you could outdraw me. Having a change of mind?"

He could see that *something* had changed in Rome. Maybe the weapon jammed into his chin or Clay's quiet sureness. Whatever, Clay decided the time was now. Jack would either back down or die. Clayton was so fed up, he didn't much care which. He still held most of his shot of whiskey in his left hand, and he proceeded to throw it in the gunman's face.

"Does this help you make up your mind, Jack?"

It started in Rome's eyes. Just a little shift to one side, as if trying to find a way out. When Clay didn't let up, his hands shook. He backed up a step, and his breath escaped in a sound that was half-hiss, half-moan. Jack wheeled around and walked through the door to the street, his chin on his chest.

Clay turned back to the bartender. "Pour me another drink. The last one got dirty." This time he knocked the whiskey back in one motion, then broke his own rule. "Another."

While he waited for it he turned to survey the room and was immediately aware of who it was that had come in while his attention was on Jack Rome.

"Remember me?" the man asked.

"Sure. I never forget a fellow who wears his gun like that." Clay indicated the .45 in a cutaway and tied-down holster. "Your name is George, isn't it?"

"Yeah, you've got me pegged. Maybe you also remember the last time we met, right down here at the other end of this bar. I told you I'd expect you to prove yourself when you were sober."

Clayton merely nodded. George went on, "I don't think one drink makes a man like you drunk. Do you?"

Somehow Clay didn't believe this fellow really wanted to fight. Something about the whole approach didn't ring true.

"I'm not drunk," Clay admitted. "On the other hand, I have trouble killing someone who hasn't done anything to me."

George grinned. "Well, I could throw a whiskey in your face like you did Jack, or I could slug you. But I don't need any of that. I only have to say you weren't drunk that other night in here, and it was very likely you that propped the drunk against the back door."

A barely perceptible twinkle in George's eyes told Clay that he wasn't about to follow up on any of those ideas. Besides, George's kind didn't talk so much, they acted.

Clay grinned in return. "Why don't I buy you a drink while we talk about it?"

George moved up beside him and leaned against the bar. "Set 'em up on me, Mart."

Clayton let his other drink sit and tried the new one. This was much better whiskey, even though he had ordered the best before. He wondered if there was some way he could use George to get a look at the others who lived up at the house on the hill with the man.

"How many live or stay up where you do?" Clay ventured.

"Oh, it varies," George said in a noncommittal tone.

Clay considered, then thought to take a chance and trust his companion. He tried again. "You may have heard that I was following a man's trail when I came here. The house on the hill is the only place I haven't looked."

George was sipping his whiskey as if he really enjoyed it. "That's real interesting, since the man sent me down tonight to find you and tell you he wants to see you."

Clayton struggled not to betray his surprise. "Now? This late?"

George smiled widely. "It's the top of the evening to the man. In fact, he never gets up until the afternoon is well along."

Clay nodded and finished his drink. George did the same, and they went out together. Clay marveled at his own thoughts on the way up the hill, since his companion said nothing and he had plenty of time to think. He had to wonder on the fact that, even more than his excitement, he looked forward to seeing the inside of that house, where every man was a gunman, and Clay could be killed for being honest and walking into a den of thieves.

He was so nervous that he turned to George and told him about the jailbreak, bringing the Rome brothers with him, and following a gambler's trail to The Settlement. Clay finished with a description of Merle Hollister.

"That's the man I'm looking for. Can you tell me if he's up here where we're going?"

His companion grinned but refused to answer. Clay gritted his teeth. It wasn't like him to permit any person or situation to get under his skin, and he said no more.

He followed George through the front door of the house on the hill. They stood in a narrow hall that looked to go the whole length of the building. George motioned to a bench against the wall.

"Wait. I'll see if he's ready for you." George disappeared through a door down at the far end of the hallway but was back in minutes. He motioned for Clay to come.

"You're on your own," he said tersely as he opened the door.

If Stoney Wall's small house was comfortable, by Clayton's standards, the man's home was grand. The first thing Clay noticed was that two walls were lined with books. The floor was covered with thick rugs. It was obvious to Clay, who'd been raised back East, that all the furniture had been freighted in. None of the usual homemade things he found out here existed in this house, that he could see. The huge fireplace in the wall threw a bright blaze of warmth into the big room.

From an easy chair came a voice Clayton knew he'd heard before. "Clay! Come in."

He looked toward the source of the voice, but the room light was too dim for him to identify the speaker as he continued. "I'm sure you remember Leon."

"Hello, Clay." Leon was sitting in a second easy chair.

Clay returned the greeting, lacking somehow in his usual confident manner of talk.

"There were several reasons why I asked you to come up, Clay," the first man said. "Please sit down."

The words were a request, but the voice was a command. Clay dropped into a third chair. He wasn't comfortable. He'd settled in so deeply that he'd be considerably slowed down if he had to draw. Working his six-gun around in his lap, he looked up and tried to identify the first voice. Before he could, the man spoke again, and now Clayton knew who was the leader of the outlaw town.

"You don't need to worry about getting to your weapon here tonight. Neither Leon nor I are armed."

Clay didn't move, determined not to give his startled feeling away. After a moment he spoke to the man. "I followed your trail from Agate to the Dry Creek Station, then here. No wonder I lost it. I hadn't thought you might be up here on the hill the whole time."

The man he knew as Merle Hollister said, "Yes. Well, I wasn't sure I wanted you to find me, but you've been doing such a good job of planning outings for the Romes that I decided to talk to you."

"I never intended to get involved in any of The Settlement's jobs," Clay quickly put in, meaning to set the record straight. "I *did* try to help Orville and Ty Rome, but only as a personal favor to them."

But the man continued, as if he wanted to finish what he'd intended to say before Clay tried to make his position clear.

"I also liked your choice of men to go along with the Romes. Besides, you're fast and smart. Altogether you're the type of man who would be on top anyplace you landed."

The unexpected praise momentarily made Clay forget that he needed Hollister to clear him of killing an old farmer, the one who had started his troubles.

Merle Hollister studied his face and added, "Leon holds the same opinion."

Clayton looked from one to the other and grimly set his jaw, determined to reveal no more of his emotions.

The man spoke to him again. "Clay, I've been curious as to just why you were following me."

"You seem to know so much, I thought you would have figured that out, too."

"No, I don't know everything," Hollister said, shaking his head. "I'd like you to start at the beginning and tell it all. Every detail."

Clay sat with his head down for a minute. Then he talked for a long time, explaining from when he first met Mary Ward up to his meeting in the bar with Jack Rome. The only thing he left out was the intimacy of the last time he'd been with Betsey McKenna. Even now that memory brought a pleasurable tingle to his loins.

When he stopped talking, a brief silence fell. The man asked, "Why did you decide only tonight that you really didn't need Jack Rome to clear you of murdering the deputy?"

"I'm ashamed to admit it," Clay answered. "But I didn't realize until tonight that Jack killed Sid Ryder while his two brothers and I were together, and *they* could alibi me."

Merle nodded slowly. "They might just do it, Clay. Neither gets along very well with Brother Jack. On the other hand, I very much doubt that either would go to any lawman to testify on your behalf, since they're also wanted."

Clay had to admit it was true. But he added, "That's still a better chance than Jack clearing me."

"It wouldn't do you any good unless you could get me to clear you of the first murder," Hollister pointed out.

"I know," Clay said reluctantly, "but I thought you were only a gambler. I didn't realize the full scope of your activities." He ventured a rueful smile. "You could go to Agate as the gambler, just as you were the night I first met you. They wouldn't have to know all the rest."

Now it was the man's turn to smile. "I could, but what's in it for me? If you were cleared of both murders, I'd lose your ability to plan and, therefore, most likely have that much less income."

Clay's mind raced. What could he do? Would he have to give up, after all? No, by God! he told himself. He'd come too far. There *had* to be a way.

His thoughts were interrupted by Leon as he rose from his chair and said, "Looks like you two are at an impasse. In my book that always calls for a drink. Will you both join me?"

Not waiting for an answer, Leon quickly served drinks and directed the conversation to more general topics. Time passed pleasantly for Clay, and despite their different objectives, he found that he and the man got along. They talked well into the night, long after Leon must have left. Each showed surprise at how widely the other had read, although Clayton figured all the books along each wall should have told him something about Hollister.

Merle relaxed bit by bit and told Clay things he obviously didn't discuss with the others. Clay couldn't figure out why, yet in a way it seemed almost natural. In return he found himself telling the man details of his growing up that he couldn't remember thinking about in years.

Clay mulled it all over on the way back to his camp. It came to him that he'd mentioned Betsey several times, and that she'd completely taken over the place Mary Ward had held in his heart. Merle Hollister must have known this, too. He must have known several things about Clayton's deepest needs, and yet he'd agreed to nothing.

The eastern horizon was turning gray when Clay rolled in his blanket, confused, but needful of whatever sleep he could get.

Chapter Ten

****

Clay woke to find Hank sitting nearby. "Morning, Clay. Been waiting for you. Didn't want to come too close and wake you up."

Clayton sat up and strapped his gun belt on, then put on his hat and pulled on his boots. "Good morning, Hank, if it *is* still morning. The sun looks to be halfway up the sky already. I haven't slept this late since I don't know when."

Hank nodded, then came right to the point. "I been thinkin' on it a lot. Reckon I want to try a-livin' at the way station. If that feller McKenna really wants me, it couldn't be no worse than here. Only, if you stayed here and couldn't come to visit, it might get kind of lonesome. Like it was before you came."

"That's great news, Hank, and you know I'll come when I can. But we can't go right away. It would be better to wait until things cool down after what happened there the other night."

"Yeah, well, I ain't in no hurry, but it's something to hope for."

"Good, Hank, but you know what? I've talked all night and slept late, and now I'm awake with an empty stomach. Let's go see if the fellow who runs the eating place will feed us."

They went. On the way Hank told Clay, "I heard about you backing old Jack Rome down last night. It's all over this place. Seems like the only thing there is to talk about."

Clay shook his head. "I hadn't intended to do anything like that, but he just kept ragging me. I finally realized there was no reason to take it anymore."

"Ain't nobody seen Jack since he left the saloon last night, either. Me, I don't care if I never see him again."

Over the next few days Clay heard regular reports on Jack Rome, but neither he nor Hank saw the gunman. Jack was said to come to the store or the saloon or the eatery at odd hours, when the fewest people were likely to be around. Everybody supposedly left him completely alone except for one man, a thin fellow with a squeaky voice. From the description, Clay thought he recalled this man as sitting at the table with Grover when Clay first came to The Settlement.

This thin man was reported to be Jack's line of communication with the rest of the outlaw town and the apparent source of the rumors about a job Rome was planning. Jack allegedly had said he'd take care of Clay when the job was done.

Hank listened and repeated all these tidbits to Clay, but Clay himself paid little attention. He had been sure that he and Merle Hollister would talk again and had kept his thoughts on that possibility. When it didn't happen right away, he was still reluctant to go up to the house himself and ask to see the man.

Instead, he let the days slip by while he took care of the horses in the pasture and sneaked in some target practice. After a while he got to thinking about the Rome brothers and realized he'd lost track of how long it had been since they'd left on the job to relieve the wagon train of its gold. Then one day, coming back from breakfast, Clay saw them at their old camping place, sound asleep.

When he got to the pasture he found their packhorse with galled places where the saddle had rubbed him raw. Clay worked most of the morning, trying to heal the results of overloading the animal for too long a time. At last he finished and went again to the Romes' camp, thinking to offer to buy them a meal in return for learning how their job had gone.

As Clay got close he could see Orville sitting alone by a small fire, drinking coffee. Orville turned and saw him, jumping to his feet and holding out his hand while he grinned.

"Clay, am I glad to be back! That trip was real work."

Clayton looked around. He could see several bedrolls scattered, with weapons nearby. Then his eye caught a small canvas-covered mound in the center of the camp.

"It's funny in a way," Orville was saying. "We ride into an outlaw town with the biggest haul ever seen in these parts. Everybody goes right to sleep and for the first time in days doesn't post a guard."

Clay stared pointedly at the pile. "Then your trip was successful?"

"You bet. Come look. There was more gold than we were expecting."

Some doubt must have shown on Clay's face, for Orville Rome continued, "Here, I'll show you." He went over and yanked the cover off the top of the pile.

Clay saw a packsaddle and a pair of saddlebags, all bulging.

"Every one is plumb full of gold," Orville said. He proceeded to open the topmost bag, reaching inside with both hands. Making a great show of it, he pulled out a bar full of dull metal that was obviously heavy.

Clay looked hard. "I always thought that gold was shiny bright."

Orville laughed. "Scratch the surface, and it is. I had a hard time convincing a couple of these boys"—he indicated his sleeping men—"that it really was gold. They thought it was some kind of decoy."

While he and Orville Rome talked, Clay pulled his knife from his belt and scraped the blade across the side of the bar. Sure enough, the flakes he caught in his hand and the patch where he had chipped were both a gleaming luster. The two continued talking until a couple of the other men woke up. Clayton began to wonder if his friend had any idea as to the value of the gold, when Orville asked him to go along to see Stoney Wall.

"I should take this to him myself, but it's heavy. I'd have to get the packhorse back, and, truth to tell, I'd hate to load him again," Orville said.

Clay nodded. "Sure. I'll go. I've already seen the back of that poor horse."

It came to him that Orville had been talking faster than usual, and he wondered if it was due to excitement over the big take. He walked with Orville, and as they approached Stoney's cabin they could see somebody sitting on the porch. The person got up to note who they were, and it turned out to be Beef. When he made sure of the pair he went into the house.

Orville Rome never noticed. He was busy talking about the holdup, and every time he went over it he added more detail and made the work of moving the gold seem harder and harder.

"It was heavy," Orville reiterated. "But it wasn't that so much as it was protecting it. I wasn't too sure of some of the men, so either Ty or I always had to be awake."

They reached Stoney's front door. As Orville raised his hand to knock, it was opened from the inside. Beef hulked there, and for a minute Clay thought he meant to deny them entrance. Then he moved aside and waved them in.

Orville brushed past the big man and headed excitedly toward the desk Stoney normally sat behind. He stopped, temporarily confused, when Wall's chair was empty. Turning, he looked at Clay, then Beef. The big guard scowled. Clayton signaled Orville with a glance toward the fireplace, where Stoney sat.

Clay made to speak, but Orville rushed in ahead. "By God," he said, "you wouldn't believe the amount of gold we brought back."

Stoney smiled slowly. "Tell me about it. Convince me."

Orville Rome quickly made his point. He hadn't gone far before Stoney interrupted to ask where the gold was and how many guards were watching it.

When he heard that it was in a pile at the Romes' camp with only two tired men guarding it, he ordered Beef, "Get two or three men from up on the hill to come and take over the guard duty. Have the rest set up a way to count and measure. We need an accurate idea as to the value of what the Romes have here."

He turned to Clay. "Get a couple of men you can trust to help with the heavy work of moving this stuff."

Orville looked from one to the other, not as sure of himself as he had been. Clay looked back at him and requested, "Come help me, Orville."

They went to work. With Stoney in charge and Clay handling the men who were doing the heavy lifting, Orville and Ty Rome soon felt pushed aside and left out. They stood on the side and talked quietly among themselves and one or two of the men who had gone out on the job with them. Clay noticed and went over as soon as he got a chance.

Without preamble Ty demanded, "Now that you and Stoney have took over our gold, will me and Orville and our boys get a fair deal?"

Clay was taken aback. He'd never before heard even a hint of hostility from the big man. But, he reflected, he shouldn't have been surprised. Gold did strange things to men, making enemies out of friends. People killed one another for much less than what was involved here. But he also understood their misgivings that the gunmen from the house on the hill might intend to take it all and leave the Romes and himself without a share.

His own feelings surprised him. Clay *wanted* a share, but up until now he'd thought he didn't care all that much. He said, "I think we'll all be treated fairly, Ty. But, just in case, let's be prepared for anything we'd have to do if they try to cheat us."

It was Orville who nodded and answered. "There are a couple of men who went with us that can be trusted. I'll talk to them."

Clay knew the situation was explosive. "Tell them to be careful. Let's not start anything unless we have to, but spread out, just in case. Don't anybody jump the gun. If it has to be done, let me be the one to make the decision. All right?"

Orville nodded immediately, and Clay turned to his brother. Ty didn't hesitate. "Fine by me."

Clayton walked to his right, looking around to discover that most of the men from The Settlement had come to see what was going on. Orville Rome was talking to a pair of men who had been with him on the raid, and Ty was in conversation with still another. Clay stopped with his back to a large tree and waited.

Turning his head slightly, he was truly surprised to see that Merle Hollister had come down and was standing silently. Something seemed different about the man, and at first Clay couldn't define it. Then it dawned on him that Merle was wearing a pair of tied-down six-guns.

A tension filled the air, not unlike the pressure that built prior to a violent thunderstorm. Others seemed to sense it, too, Clay thought. With his back to the tree, he was on the west side of where the gold was being measured and loaded. He made up one side of a loose rectangle. On his left, the south side, were the Romes and their crew.

To his right were Stoney, Leon, Beef, and the man. Across from Clay were the outlaws from town. He thought that most of them couldn't realize how much was involved here. Still, they had to have *some* idea, or they wouldn't have all gotten there so fast. Somehow the smell of gold had brought them to the Romes' camp in the middle of the day.

Gunplay and fast death might have exploded at any moment, but the man had it all in his grasp. He raised his voice only a little. "Orville, Ty. Will you and your men take paper money for your gold?"

Both said they would, and their crew agreed. With one question Hollister had allied three sides of the rectangle against the fourth. Everyone turned toward the fellows who had come from the saloon as Hollister directed, "You men go back to your drinks and card games. What happens here is no concern of yours."

The men from the town muttered slightly among themselves but began to drift back the way they had come.

When all the gold was weighed and loaded, Merle Hollister faced those who had a share coming. "There is so much gold in these bars that I know of no way to sell it, only to someone with a crusher and smelter. That way it can be mixed in with the regular ore. Then the man who owns the smelter can sell it with his."

Everyone listened closely. The man continued, "But we have a problem. The only fellow I know who does that kind of job will pay but ten dollars an ounce."

Clay figured quickly in his head that the owner of the smelter must double his money. But Hollister was speaking again. "After my usual cut, the balance is still so much that the only way I can pay all of you is if some will take a bank draft."

One of the crew spoke out. "I don't want no bank draft. Onliest time I was ever in a bank, the man in charge commenced to shootin' at me, and I had to kill him."

This could be bad, Clayton saw. He said, "I'd *rather* have a bank draft, if it's good anywhere. It'd purely be easier to carry around."

The man nodded his thanks, and the Romes followed Clay's lead. "You can make out one bank draft for me and Ty," Orville said.

The one who had wanted only cash asked how many shared. Merle shot a quick look at Orville Rome, who answered, "One share for each of you here. Clay, Ty, and I get two. This was all agreed to, if you remember, before you signed on for the job."

"Damn!" the fellow blasted back. "That was afore we knowed how big this here job was. How much does one share come to?"

The man himself had been doing some figures, and he soon had an answer. "Each single share is four thousand five hundred dollars."

The amount staggered some of the onlookers and more than satisfied the testy fellow. Merle Hollister began calmly paying off the people who wanted only cash. Some wanted it all in coin, while others were willing to accept paper money. When it came to the Romes, the man asked if a draft on a San Francisco bank would do. They were happy with that, because they said that was where they were going.

Hollister turned to Clay and asked him where he was going, the man's eyes grave and dark.

"I've not made any plans," Clayton returned. "But it would most likely be somewhere in open, less-settled country."

Merle said nothing else but gave him a draft on a Denver bank.

Finally it was all taken care of. The gold was hauled up to the house on the hill, and the men who had helped went on their separate ways. Hank suddenly appeared, and Clay knew he must have been watching the whole deal from a distance.

Clayton turned to grin at the kid. "What do you think, Hank? There's enough here to stock a good-sized ranch." He waved the bank draft.

Hank's thin face was split by the biggest smile Clay had ever seen on him. "Let's do it, Clay. We could go down to that place I heard a couple of the fellers a-talking about. New Mexico. What happened up here wouldn't mean nothin' down there."

Hank's idea gave him another thought, and he put it in motion right away.

"Hank, let's ride to the Dry Creek Station tomorrow and talk to Walt and Betsey."

The kid watched him as if trying to figure out exactly what he was thinking. Clay continued, "It would be best if we left shortly after midnight, rested someplace during the day tomorrow, and rode in there after dark tomorrow night."

Hank looked hard at Clay for a couple of seconds, then said, "I'll get things ready and catch me some sleep so's I can be ready when you call me."

He started away, then turned back with one more question. "Should I take all my belongings?"

Clay made to answer but was interrupted as three horses rode straight into Orville's camp and skidded to a halt. Jack Rome leaped off his mount in an obvious fury and began to shout at his brothers.

"What's this I hear about you made a big haul and didn't cut me in?"

Clay backed up a step to keep Jack and his two riders all in sight. He eyed the one he thought of as Squeaky, who reportedly had been Rome's only confidant after the saloon showdown. Clay wondered who the third man was. He sat a big horse and appeared to *need* a stronger mount than an ordinary rider.

The fellow filled a regular stock saddle to overflowing. He wasn't big across the shoulders, but below the belt he ballooned out. The most noticeable thing about him was the double-barreled scattergun he held in front of him. At present it wasn't pointed at anyone, but just the fact that he had it in his hands made him a force to be reckoned with.

Jack continued to harangue Orville and Ty. "It's this damned Clay feller. Ever since he came along I ain't been good enough for my own brothers. Well, dammit, I ain't a-going to put up with it no longer. There's three of us here, and I intend to get even for all that bastard has done to me since we got out of that jail in Agate."

"Now, Jack," Orville tried to reason with his younger

brother. "It's not right to blame your troubles on Clay. Why, we'd all three have hanged if he'd not come along and got us out of there."

"The hell we would. I could of gone up through the ceiling and into the office and got out just as good without him."

Clay could see it was useless to try to enlighten Jack with the truth. He was only going to believe what he'd convinced himself of. Orville was talking now, but Clay wasn't listening. He thought it prudent to keep track of Jack Rome's cronies but found he was already a bit late. The skinny one with the squeaky voice had palmed his six-gun and was pointing it at Clay.

Jack cut in on what his brother was saying. "SHUT UP!" he roared. When he had everyone's attention he looked to the bigger of his two riders.

"Keep my brothers covered. Don't shoot 'em; they ain't either one of 'em dumb enough to try anything while you got 'em covered with that scattergun."

Moving only his eyes, Clayton tried to find out what had happened to Hank. He hoped the kid had sense enough to get clear.

Jack Rome faced Clay with a murderous glare. "I'm goin' to kill you real slow. I'll enjoy every minute of it."

Something moved at the edge of Clay's field of vision. He tried to look without betraying to Jack or his men that there was anything behind them. It was Hank, bending over to pick an object up off the ground. He straightened up, holding on to a short-barreled carbine, one that a member of Orville's crew must have left behind.

Taking two steps to his left as Rome paused to gulp in a deep breath, Hank worked the lever and jacked a shell into the chamber. The sound was unmistakable. Jack and his pair of riders froze.

Hank's voice was strong and confident. "Now, you yahoos just let your weapons down real easy, and I won't have to kill any of you."

Surprisingly, at least to Clay, the skinny fellow showed the most gumption. "I don't think so, kid. They's three of us and only one of you. Chances are, you ain't never killed before. I'm bettin' I can turn and fire whilst you're makin' up your mind."

But Hank hadn't lived amid the hard kind of men who inhabited The Settlement without learning some. "Thanks, Squeaky, now I know which one to cut down first. You'd lose that bet. I think I can get you, and your friend with the shotgun is going to die, too. Because whether he goes for Orville and Ty or tries for Clay, the other will take him."

Jack Rome just stood there. The wild and shifty look was back in his eyes, stronger than it had been that night in the saloon. The big man with the shotgun was the first to give up. He let the hammers down on both barrels and said, "I always figgered I knew when it was time to throw in a hand."

He let the scattergun slide down until he held it by the barrel with his right hand. Then he leaned over slowly and dropped it to the ground. He raised his hands above his head, kneed his mount around, and walked him away.

Squeaky dropped his gun into leather and turned toward Hank. "I'll remember you, kid, believe me, I will," he growled. His horse followed the big man's.

All eyes shifted to look at Jack, who had been watching Hank. Now he looked at Clay but didn't like what he saw in Clayton's face. He turned instead to his brothers.

"Orville!" Jack said. "You were goin' to give me a share, weren't you? Hell, I know you done the job. But I'm your brother, and I'd of been glad to go and help bring the gold back." His voice took on a pleading quality. "Why didn't you ask me to help?"

Clay found himself comparing this groveling excuse for a man with the blustering gunman who used to be Jack Rome. He wondered if he was responsible for the change, then answered his own question: there was no more backbone in the man Jack used to be than in the one who stood here now.

Orville turned away wordlessly and started on the task of cleaning up the campsite. But being ignored only made Jack worse.

"Ty!" Jack said, and would have gone on, but his other brother turned his back. Rome looked quickly to Clay and Hank as they both left and started toward the horse corral.

Suddenly Jack's bluster came back. "Good!" he yelled. "I don't need any of you bastards. I can get my own outfit of men and do my own job. I'll bring back more loot than you did."

His voice rose to a scream. "Goddamn you all to hell! I'm better than all of you put together. I'll show you. I'll show the whole bunch of you."

By dawn of the next day, Clay and Hank were camped well away from The Settlement. They hadn't had much time to talk since they'd walked away from a raving Jack Rome.

As Hank pulled off his boots he said, "Boy, that feels good. I bet I'll sleep right through till dark."

Clay grinned. "Go ahead. I'll keep watch now, but maybe you'd better watch awhile this afternoon so I can at least get a couple of hours."

"Sure, I wasn't thinkin'. It's just that I never slept as much as I'd planned."

"Why not? Did you have trouble getting to sleep early?"

"Well, last night I went up to the waterfall just at dark, wantin' a quick swim before I tried to sleep some. On the way back as I passed the saloon I could hear Jack's voice. I slipped up close to the bat-wings to find out what kind of lies he was a-telling now."

"Anything I should know about?"

Hank stretched out and yawned as he pulled a light blanket over himself. "Ain't sure. I couldn't hear good. I tried to stand on my tiptoes, but I still couldn't see over the bat-wings. So I hunkered down and peeped under. Jack was a-standing there with his back to me, and them other two was with him. They were tryin' to get fellers to go out with them on some job or another.''

Clay finished rubbing down the buck and started on the gray. ''How many men did he want? Did he get them?''

''I couldn't hear as to how many Jack thought he needed. He *did* get three or four, the ones that don't go out on many jobs 'cause nobody wants 'em.''

''Where was this job?''

''Never found that out, neither.''

Clay sighed, feeling sorry for anyone who got in Jack Rome's way. It was just too easy for Jack to kill.

Chapter Eleven

****

It was well past full dark when Clay and Hank pulled across the dry creek bed from the way station.

They dismounted, and Clay said, "You stay with the horses. Keep them quiet. I'll slip up to the station and find out if it's safe for us to go in."

Hank grasped the strap of Clay's mounts in answer. Clayton liked to travel with a spare horse on the lead behind him. By changing his saddle regularly he didn't wear out either mount, and he covered ground faster than most riders. Before leaving The Settlement he'd made sure that Hank had an extra horse as well. Now the kid led the four horses to a small patch of grass close to the edge of the creek bank.

Clayton gave the stable a wide berth. He wasn't sure as to whether Blondy might still be there, and he didn't want the horses in the corral to scent him and announce his arrival. When he was well past that danger, he could see a dim light at the back of the station house. Knowing that this must be the kitchen, he figured Betsey might be there, and he headed that way.

Slowly, one step at a time, he went to the window. He stood next to it, then leaned far enough to see that Betsey was, indeed, finishing the kitchen work for the day. So far, so good! But he still didn't know if there was an overnight guest at the station, or if Blondy might be in the front room.

Clay made a complete circuit of the building. He found a light on in the front room but couldn't get close enough to see in without crossing the porch. Not about to do that, because he knew he couldn't move noiselessly, he went back to the kitchen window.

He pondered. Should he take a chance and knock at the back door? Or should he walk in and hope that Betsey wouldn't give him away when he surprised her? Clay looked in the window again. Betsey was just picking up the dishpan of dirty water, and he remembered that she always carried the water out to dump it at the base of one of the trees. Here on the high plains, what few trees grew needed all the water they could get.

The door opened. Betsey McKenna walked out, carrying the pan. Clay waited until she reached the trees. Then, hoping not to startle her, he quietly spoke her name.

Betsey jerked around to face him. At the same time, something about his voice must have registered, for she asked, "Clay? Is that you?"

He took two steps and reached for her. The dishpan clattered to the ground.

A short time later they sat around the table in the kitchen with Walt and Hank. McKenna explained that he'd had to fire his hostler. Blondy had been neglecting his work to spend most of his time spying on Walt and Betsey. When the stationmaster called him on it, Blondy had let it slip that he was hoping to catch Clay there and collect the reward.

Betsey finished the story. "So now Uncle has to do all the work of preparing the teams, and I've taken over the record keeping."

Clay glanced up to see Hank looking at him as if he wanted to speak, and he nodded at the kid. Hank blurted, "I could stay and help get the teams ready."

Walt and Betsey both grinned. "Hank," Clay questioned, "did you leave much back at The Settlement?"

"Naw, nothin' I care about. Got all my money on me, and I rode my bay. Only thing is the second horse you had me bring. That copper dun don't belong to me. Good as he is, he'll be missed."

Clay said, "I'll take him back and leave my buckskin here. I'll also take the gray to ride back."

He hesitated, not sure how to bring up the real reason for this visit. Then he plunged ahead. "Walt, Betsey. How would you like to go someplace away from here and start a ranch?"

McKenna stared, then let a gust of air escape from between his lips. "It'd be great, Clay, only it takes a pile of money to do that kind of thing."

"Well," Clayton said, keeping a straight face. "How would you feel about a partner who put up the money, but spent most of his time away from the ranch? Trying to make sure the law wouldn't ever come looking for him?"

Betsey sat very still as she studied Clay, her big dark eyes burning out of a suddenly pale face. Walt looked hard at him, frowning. Then, as if the whole thing came clear all at once, his frown turned into a big smile.

Walt reached out as if to shake hands on a deal. "How much cash are we talking about?"

But Betsey broke in with, "Clay! How clean is this money? If you suddenly have a large amount, and you've been living at the outlaw town . . ."

She hesitated, unsure of herself. "I don't know, Clay. I guess what I really want to ask is if there's blood on this money. Did you help steal it? And, if not, how do you come to have so much?"

Clay removed the draft from his inside pocket and put it in the center of the table. He faced Betsey, took both her hands in his, and spoke. "First, there's no blood on it. I wasn't there when the former owner was relieved of the gold that paid for this draft on a Denver bank." He blew out a gust of air as he searched for the right words. "I *did* do some valuable work for the men who led the raid. And I don't see how my bank draft could ever be traced to that holdup."

He wanted to convince her, above all else, but didn't know what else to say. As he hesitated, Betsey put in, "Of course, it's up to Uncle." Her voice trailed off.

The thought came to Clay that at least she didn't seem to want to close the door. Maybe that would be enough, sometime in the future.

Walt McKenna made his feelings clear. "If you tell me the money has no blood on it and that you, yourself, had no hand in the actual holdup, Clay, then I don't care where it came from."

He looked from Clayton to Betsey to Hank. When no one spoke, Walt went on as if it was all settled. "Do you have somewhere in mind to start this ranch, Clay, or are you going to leave it up to me?"

Clay turned to Walt. Somehow, for the first time ever, he was glad it wasn't Betsey he was facing just at this moment. "I have no firm plans. But Hank said something just the other day that made me think of the New Mexico territory, and I asked some questions of an old outlaw who used to be a trapper. He told me that there are thousands of acres of grass down there, just waiting for cows to drop calves on it and turn all that grass into beef."

He grinned at Hank and said to Walt, "Part of the deal is that you take on my friend, here, as top hand. He might even be a help in finding just the right place to start this cattle empire."

As soon as Clay stopped talking, Hank spoke up. "I'd work hard, and wouldn't either of you be sorry that I went along. Some other feller *I* heard a-talking about New Mexico said the Rio Grande River runs right through. And I thought a big river like that'd sure have a lot of little streams a-running into it."

He caught his breath and continued, "So that's where you should look for us when you get your name cleared, Clay."

McKenna put in, "Not so fast there, young man. I can't just pull up stakes here and leave the stage company in the lurch. It might take them a month or more to find somebody to run this place."

Clay smiled. "I don't think that'll be a problem, Walt. Just so you get well along the way before winter."

Clay felt a sudden relief wash over him. Hank was safely out of The Settlement. He knew who the gambler was and that the McKennas would not come to trouble. It was only a matter of time, he felt sure, until he could find a way to clear himself of both murders. He could go back to the outlaw town and concentrate all his efforts on Merle Hollister and the Rome brothers.

Later that night as Betsey and Clay lay in each other's arms, there came a banging at the front door of the station house. Only moments later the same thing was repeated at the back.

"Open up, McKenna," a voice boomed. "This is the law. Open up, I say." The pounding resumed at both doors.

Clay jumped out of bed and scrambled into his clothes. "Betsey, I'm going out the window," he whispered. "Try to give me as much time as you can. I'm glad I left the pair of horses I'm taking back down on the creek bank away from the barn and corral."

He could hear Walt McKenna stumping down the hall toward the door. "You just hold your horses a bit and don't break my door down. I'm coming."

Clay heard the bar that secured the front door drop to the floor as he crossed the room to the window. Then: "You've got that outlaw Clayton hid here someplace. My new deputy seen his buckskin horse down at the stable."

As Clay opened the window he heard Blondy's voice at the back of the building. "Open this door! How come it's latched? It was never kept fastened when I worked for you, McKenna."

Carefully, Clay stuck his head out the window and looked around. Seeing nothing, he climbed out and heard, right outside Betsey's door, Walt's angry voice. "No! Now, dammit, that's my niece's room. You can't go in there."

Betsey, sounding convincingly sleepy and confused, called out, "What's wrong, Uncle?"

Clay heard no more as he ran in a low crouch away from the station house. A few minutes later he was astride his gray and leading the copper dun, headed west toward The Settlement. He rode the gray only a short time before it came up lame. Clay slid to the ground, glad he had a second mount. He picked up the off-front foot and found a stone lodged there.

Removing the stone, Clay traded his saddle to the copper dun. It would help his gray rest the bruised hoof. By the time he finally rode into The Settlement around midnight of the following night, he had decided that the copper was the best horse he'd ever thrown a leg over.

It was barely light enough the following morning to see by when Leon visited his camp by the corral. "Come on, Clay. The man wants his best mount saddled and ready to ride by the time he finishes breakfast. When he's in a hurry, that doesn't take long."

Clay soon had a rope on the horse Leon had indicated. As he put the saddle on, Leon explained why Merle Hollister was in such an all-fired hurry.

"It's Jack Rome. He's got a bunch of no-goods together for a job and has broken the man's rules."

Clayton paused to look across the horses back at Leon.

"Don't stop," Merle's lieutenant ordered. "When he's in this mood, believe me, it doesn't do to keep him waiting. Anyhow, Jack never got his plan approved, but he *does* owe the man money. On top of that, he took this group out of here in broad daylight yesterday, and this job is too close to home. He's going to try the bank in Agate. The man never heard about it till just a little while ago. And another thing to make him testy is that he's not been to bed yet."

Leon swung into the saddle and took the mount to the

house on the hill. Clay watched him go, wondering if there was some way he could use this to his own advantage. He couldn't be sure, since he didn't know what Merle Hollister had in mind. His only hope was to go with the man. Clay wasn't sure how Hollister would take it, but he was determined to try.

While he got the gray saddled and put the copper dun on a lead, he thought about how Leon had behaved. He'd hustled like an underling afraid of his boss. Clay had never seen this attitude before in anybody at The Settlement. It put a whole new light on the man he knew as Merle Hollister.

He didn't have long to speculate on how Hollister would take to his wanting to go along. As the man started down the chute where the rocky stream ran to the place the guard was posted, Clayton dropped in behind him. The man looked back, anger plain on his face. But when he saw it was Clay, his expression changed.

All he said was, "Don't get in my way."

He rode down the stream at what Clayton considered a reckless pace. Neither spoke again until they were well away from the entrance to the valley of The Settlement. The man cut across country in what Clay thought must be a direct route to Agate.

Hollister pushed his mount hard. When he finally stopped for the horse to take a breather and drink at a small stream, he asked, "Just what do you expect to gain by following me?"

"I have an interest in both you and Jack Rome," Clay answered as he transferred his saddle to the dun. "You, maybe more than Jack. You're the only one who can clear me of the first murder."

As Clay reached under the copper to get the cinch he heard the man say, "I can go to town as a gambler and get away with it. But you, on the other hand, don't dare show yourself in Agate at all."

Merle finished talking, swung to the saddle, and spurred

away. Clay gave one more tug to the cinch, looped it back through, and climbed into the saddle. He no longer tried to match the man's pace but meant just to keep him in sight.

The town was in view the next time Merle stopped. He waited until Clay caught up, then asked as if the thought had just occurred to him, "What do you plan to do now? You're wanted bad here. In fact, I'd rather not be seen with someone whose likeness is on wanted posters around town."

Clay didn't hesitate. "I've thought about it. For one, Alf Billings, who runs the horse-trading business, wouldn't turn me in. I know for a fact he doesn't think I did either killing. He won't go against me, especially if I pay for the horses that the Romes took the night we vacated the jail."

A new thought came to the man. "While you're at it, buy me another good horse to ride away from here. Mine won't make the trip back."

That's why I bother with two at once, Clayton answered silently. Aloud he said, "My pair are still in good shape. I believe I could stay ahead of any body of horsemen that might be behind me."

Hollister looked at Clayton and said, "Well, I'll leave this black with you at the livery and go to the saloon, get started on my plan. You have your friend put my saddle on a new horse and leave it hitched in front of the saloon."

He rode on. When they came to the front of the livery, Merle got down, handed his reins to Clay, and walked up the street without another word. Clayton watched him go and wondered who the man really was and if he *had* once known Clay's family. If so, how had he gotten from an honest job in Virginia to the leadership of an outlaw town in the territory west of the States?

Clay was by no means sure of his own feelings about the man. Whenever they were together he seemed both drawn to Hollister and yet repulsed. But he jerked his thoughts back to the present. What was Merle Hollister going to do here in Agate today that would affect his future?

According to what Leon had told Clay, this was the day that Jack Rome and his men were going to rob the bank. Clay knew that the man was still furious and wondered if he was going to try to stop them single-handedly. Or maybe he would just watch to see if they were successful, then simply take what he felt was his.

The more Clay pondered it, the more he thought that the Merle Hollister he knew would do neither of these things. Yet neither would he do the only other thing that came to Clayton: go to the local law and let them take care of Jack. Still, if he *would* do it, would he also remember to clear Clay of the first murder, where the whole business had started?

He shrugged and turned his mount into the big barn doors. Clay stayed in the saddle, wanting to be sure that Alf Billings himself was there, not some out-of-work cowboy that Alf was paying a small sum to watch the place while he went to eat.

The sound of so many shod hooves on the planks of the walkway brought the older man out of his office. "Yessir. You want all four of 'em grained when they've got cooled and been rubbed down?"

Then he got near enough to recognize Clay. "Damn me, boy! You hadn't ought to be here. Half this town wants to see you strung up."

"But not you, right, Alf?" Clay asked his old friend as he swung down from the saddle.

The horse trader's answer came back sure and clear. "I know you, boy. You never killed no old sodbuster or no unarmed deputy."

Clay nodded his thanks and started to speak, but Alf cut him off. "On the other hand, they was an amount still owed on that gray you got there."

Clay reached for the well-filled wallet that had been Sweeney's. "Here's your money. If I remember, it was ten dollars. And, while I'm at it, it's only fair that I pay you for the six horses the Romes took that night."

He began to count bills into the trader's hand until Alf said, "Here, that's aplenty."

"One more thing," Clay added. "How much for the very best mount you've got on hand right now?"

The old man's eyes lighted up. "They's a red sorrel in the second corral that beats any hoss I ever owned. Now, I know that some fellers don't like to ride a mare. But I tell you, boy, this'un will beat anything on four legs."

"How much?" Once again Clay counted paper money into Alf's hand. He stopped once and looked up, but Alf said, "She cost me more'n that."

Clay added two more bills, and the old man said, "If she's for you, boy, that'll do."

Clay laid on one more, then told Billings about putting the man's saddle on the new horse and leaving it hitched at the saloon. He finished by saying, "I'd like to stay here in your barn out of sight for a while, if you don't mind."

"You stay as long as you like." Alf was in good spirits. After all, he'd just taken more money in the last few minutes than he usually got in a month.

He went out to the second corral and brought back the sorrel. Alf set about changing Merle Hollister's saddle from the black to the sorrel.

As Clay looked her over, Billings said, "You can use my barn, boy. Onliest thing is, don't get yourself caught. They'll string you up quick if you show your face."

"I'll be careful," Clay promised as his mind returned to the gambler and the question of how he was going to stop Jack. The man had gone to the gaming tables as if sure he could do whatever he intended to do from there.

As Alf Billings started away with the sorrel, Clay asked, "Does the new lawman like to play poker?"

The old trader must have misunderstood. "No need to worry about him comin' here to look for you, boy. He spends a sight more time at the poker table than he does at his office."

Nonetheless, the answer gave Clay what he needed to know.

Clayton took care of the horses, making sure that each was rubbed down and had water and grain. But he left his saddle on. With one quick jerk on the cinch he could tighten it and be in the saddle and moving. He put the man's black in the darkest stall he could find, then settled down to keep watch.

The livery was located at the very edge of town. By some chance or mistake, the builder hadn't gotten it square with the rest of Agate. Or perhaps it had been there first, and the rest of the town hadn't been constructed squarely with the livery. At any rate, the slight angle allowed Clay to stand in the shadows just inside the big barn door that faced the town. From here he could watch the main street.

Clay felt fairly safe here. No one could come from town without his seeing them. If somebody came the other way, as he and Hollister had, they'd be out of sight until they were actually in the stable. But then Clay would hear their approach in time to get out of the way.

Across from the livery was a fenced pasture that Alf used when he had stock that he wanted to hold for a while. In back was a series of corrals that always held some stock, as well. A man would have a hard time getting in that way without making a disturbance.

As he watched, Clay could see Merle's new mount tied in front of the only saloon, about halfway along this same side of the street. Across the way and only a little farther along was the jail. Clay wondered how they had repaired the ceiling. Most likely, they'd done it so that a prisoner would find it difficult to get out that way again.

At the far end of town was the bank Jack Rome meant to hit and in between, the stores and businesses.

Time dragged heavily for Clayton. He found it hard to stay alert in the afternoon heat and began to feel sleepy even though he knew the barn was cooler than outside in the sun would have been. Clay reflected that Jack must be thinking to take the bank just at closing, not too bad an idea if his timing was perfect.

He thought of Betsey and Walt McKenna and Hank making the long trip to the New Mexico territory. Clay wished he could get his name cleared and go along. He'd like to have a hand in finding the ranch site and building something new, something any man could be proud of.

As he mused, time passed. He almost missed the movement when it came. Three men walked out of the saloon. One had a star pinned to his vest, and one was a definite stranger to Clay. The third was Blondy, Walt's former hostler. The stranger went toward the jail. Blondy began going from store to store. The deputy cut toward the bank.

Merle Hollister stepped through the saloon's bat-wings to watch. Clay figured he'd managed to tip off the law without getting himself involved. After the deputy had entered the bank, Blondy had disappeared into the dry goods store; the stranger had continued to remain inside the jail building; Merle turned to look toward the livery. It seemed like he was wondering if Clay was still there.

Clayton couldn't see anyone else the whole length of the street. He stepped just outside the barn door, then immediately backed into the shadows again. The man turned the other way, but somehow Clay knew Hollister had spotted him.

Clay stood quietly and watched as people now came out and made preparations along the street. It was as if Agate was expecting to be marauded from the outside. Men with rifles stationed themselves on roofs of buildings behind high false fronts and also in doorways.

An old wagon was left alongside the road just past the bank. Clay assumed it would be pushed into the street to block the robbers' going back the way they had come. If Jack Rome and his followers came into town and entered the bank, they'd have to surrender or die.

During the preparations, Alf Billings walked out of the saloon and happened to stand beside Hollister as they watched the activity. The deputy came back and spoke briefly to them. Alf nodded several times in quick succession, and Merle broke into the conversation. The deputy seemed to agree with him and went on checking the placement of people on the street.

The man untied his new sorrel from the hitch rack. He and Billings started down the street toward the livery. When they arrived, the trader gave Clay a searching look but said nothing. He waited for Hollister.

Merle said, "Clay, the deputy has everything set up. If none of these locals get trigger-happy and fire too soon, we'll both be rid of Jack Rome once and for all. He'll either be dead or in prison."

Once again Alf Billings looked from one to the other. Then he shook his head as if to say, no, he wasn't about to ask. What he *did* say was, "I witnessed a deposition this here gambler signed to the effect that you was playing cards with him when that old farmer got killed."

A big grin split Clay's face. He turned to Merle Hollister and grabbed his hand. "Thanks, thanks a lot! That's one load off my mind. Now, if I can just get Orville or Ty to do the same for me on the murder of Sid Ryder, I can go back to living a normal life."

The man shot a granite look at Clayton. "They'll be harder than I was."

Alf looked at them both a long minute, then headed for his small office, saying, "When it's time for me to help, call me."

Hollister got his rifle from his saddle boot and jacked a shell into the chamber. Any conversation between him and Clay died as they stood and waited.

Clayton had looked up toward the other end of the street for so long that he wasn't sure of what he saw when it *did* happen. At least, not until the deputy came out of the bank and waved his bandanna. All the people in sight along the street soon disappeared. Clay then saw a cloud of dust.

He advised Merle, "Time to call Alf."

Hollister leaped to his feet and stuck his head into the office doorway. "They're coming."

Seven riders pounded furiously into the far end of town from the livery. They skidded their mounts to a stop in front of the bank. Five of the crew went in while one stayed at the hitch rail in front. The last crossed the street and turned to watch the front of the bank.

Clay felt his heart beating at a crazy rate. He glanced at the man, who was peering through squinted eyes at the goings-on. As Clay turned again to look at the other end of the street, he noticed that four men were pushing the empty wagon into the road just past the bank.

The fellow in front of the bank as well as the one across the street were too intent on watching the door to see the vehicle being placed across their escape route. Then events began to happen, one so close behind the other, that Clay couldn't sort them out until afterward.

First came a shot from inside the bank. The outlaw from across the street started to double back to the hitch rail where he'd left his horse with the others. The four at the wagon heaved it over on its side, blocking the street. The man guarding the mounts in front of the bank heard the wagon's crash, turned, and commenced firing at the four barricaded behind it.

Clay thought he heard more shots from inside the bank, but suddenly there was so much gunplay that he wasn't sure of anything. Men burst out the front door and ran into a hail of lead. Only one of the would-be bank robbers managed to mount his horse. He turned and sank his spurs into the animal's flank.

Clayton saw a magnificent horse running down the main street toward him, and he thought of old tales of men running the gauntlet in an Indian village. He realized that Merle had stepped outside the door of the stable and was leveling his rifle at the horseman. Clay looked more closely and saw that it was Jack Rome.

Despite the fact that the target was moving, it was an easy mark as it approached the livery. Jack ran right at the man's gun. Merle shot. The force of the lead knocked Jack out of his saddle, and he slid slowly off the mount's rump. The horse galloped past, stirrups swinging. Hollister jacked another shell into the chamber and took careful aim at the body lying, unmoving, in the street. He shot once more, just to be sure, then turned back, walked calmly into the stable, and mounted the sorrel.

The man said to Clay, "Let's ride. We got what we came for, and these people will ask too many questions if we stay any longer."

He spurred his mount and rode away, with Clayton close behind. They rode well into the night, and when they stopped to camp Hollister said almost nothing. Neither did Clay feel like talking, and they rolled in their blankets.

Clay slept right off, but despite the fact that he'd ridden half the night, he was still up with the sun. He was drinking his third tinful of coffee when the man woke up, crawled out of his blanket, and poured himself a tin. Merle drank it slowly and never spoke a word. Then he poured a second and blew on it to cool it.

Finally he said, "I killed Jack partly for you, Clay. If I hadn't, you would have, and his brothers would have been that much more unlikely to clear you."

Clay scrutinized the man, not knowing how to answer. Hollister continued, "If you ever get to the point of giving up whatever you're trying to prove, you'll always be welcome at The Settlement. If you come back to stay, you come right up to my house. When I get ready to give it all up, you can take over."

Clayton threw a look at him. He wanted to ask where that

left Leon or George and the other lieutenants, not to mention Stoney Wall and Beef.

But the man quickly added, "Don't misunderstand me. If that's not what you want, you still have my blessing."

Clay was taken aback. He wasn't sure why the man spoke this way, nor what to ask to make things clear to him. But Hollister talked on.

"Your mother was a good woman, Clay. She was the daughter of a proud family. I see a lot of her in you."

Now Clay was truly confused. The man sounded like—well, hell, like a father! But why?

"Even if you *did* grow up in an orphanage," Merle explained, "you're not a bastard, Clay. Your mother and I were married. Her parents didn't approve, but they agreed she should live at home with them at first, while I was still traveling."

He stopped for a long look at his startled son. "I guess I carried it too far. But, as the saying goes, hindsight is better than foresight. There was always one more trip I needed to take, a little more profit I had to realize. Then the war started, and I couldn't get back to her. When I *could* get back to Richmond, I searched. I really did, Clay, but the city was in turmoil. I couldn't find any trace of her or her family. I knew that there was to be a baby, but I never saw you. In fact, I never knew whether you were a boy or a girl."

A long, painful pause followed. Clay was flooded with an overpowering wave of emotions. He sat still, damned if he'd betray how weak and unsure he felt. On one hand, he wanted to shoot this man who claimed to be his father. Yet he felt a crazy urge to bear hug him at the same time.

Merle rose, grabbed the pot from the hot coals, and poured into both tins. As he filled Clay's, he stared searchingly at his son, then spoke as he sat down again.

"I don't know what more to say to you. I've never apologized in my entire life, although I should have to your mother."

Clay's thoughts and feelings were so tangled that the only thing he could think to ask was, "Is your real name Merle Hollister?"

"One name is about like another out here on the high plains, Clay, but I don't suppose it matters at this point. I think I've told you I use different names in different places. But, as a matter of fact, it really is Merle Hollister."

His dark eyes looked into Clay's. "And Clayton was your mother's maiden name. So you, in fact, are not Clay Clayton. Your name is Clayton Hollister."

Clay stared back, his brown eyes just as intense in emotion, if not in color. Neither said anything for a space, then both went to speak at once. They both stopped.

"Oh, hell," Clay finally muttered, with a you-first gesture of the hand.

Hollister said, "We might as well put the best face we can on it. I realize it can't be pleasant for you, but the past is past. I'd like to let it lay and get to know you."

Clay only said, "I've always thought that a man should be held accountable for his mistakes."

In his heart he knew Merle couldn't change his past, but Clayton didn't know how he felt about having to live with it. The rest of the morning hours dragged by with little conversation. Several times he felt the man's gaze upon him, but neither spoke much. Finally, in the afternoon, Clay stretched out in the shade and went to sleep.

When he woke in the early evening, Merle was sitting with his back to Clay. He looked out across the open prairie as if keeping watch. When he heard Clay move around behind him, he came into the camp and lay down on his blanket without a word.

Clay never knew if his father fell asleep or not. He kept watch through the evening and early night and was just about to call Merle when he rose on his own.

"If we're going to enter The Settlement before daylight, we'd best get on the way," Hollister said. Then he grinned as he saw that Clay had their horses saddled and had been waiting.

He looked directly at Clay and said, "You'll do."

Still, the man didn't seem to be in a hurry to get to the outlaw town. A hint of gray light showed in the east when they passed the place where the first guard should have been. When Merle realized the post was unmanned, he swore under his breath.

There still wasn't enough light to see by when they reached the horse corral. But the gate stood open. The man paused without dismounting, squinting toward the few buildings of The Settlement.

Clay rode up beside and said, "Something is wrong here." It wasn't a question.

"Yes," Hollister agreed. "It's a different kind of quiet."

They rode at a slow walk toward the town, rounding the corner into the short street. Both horses shied. Right there, in the middle of their way, was a dead man. He lay on his back, sightless eyes looking up to the morning sky. Clay recognized him as one of the outlaws he'd seen around there. He looked about to find several bodies scattered along the street.

Clay sat his horse in disbelief. After what seemed like a long time the man said, "I always knew it could happen. It must have been the law. A shootout among the men would have left *some* survivors, at least."

The pair walked their mounts along the street. Halfway to the saloon they both pulled up, listening. Somebody was singing. Clay could just barely make out the words to an old camp song.

Hollister said, "Whoever it is, he's in the saloon."

They looped their reins over the rail and carefully entered the drinking place. Little light had come into the room yet. Clay located the fellow more by following his voice than by trusting his own sight.

"Tenting tonight, tenting on the old campground," the fellow sang in a quaver.

Clayton found a candle behind the bar and lighted it. Carrying it with him, he walked along the rear wall until he found his friend Davis sitting in a pool of his own blood.

At first Clay thought Davis hadn't seen him. But he broke off his song and said, "I began to think wasn't anybody goin' to find me before I passed on."

Hollister came up and looked him over. "Was it lawmen?"

Davis nodded weakly and spoke in a slow voice, now barely loud enough to hear. "Federal marshals with a bunch of bounty hunters along."

"How did they get past the guard?" the man asked.

Davis's cough left bloody bubbles on his lips. Clay leaned closely to hear. "That fellow named Porky came back, after all. He was leading 'em."

When Clay straightened up to repeat to the man what Davis had said, his dying friend grasped his arm. "The ones that surrendered was hauled off to jail," he whispered.

"What happened to the Romes?" Clayton questioned.

But Davis had lost interest in Clay. He lapsed into singing again, one syllable at a time, and almost under his breath. When he finished the last words of the song, he slid sideways and lay still.

Hollister wasn't long in making a decision. "Drag all the dead men who are out in the open into buildings and set the town afire, Clay. Then come up to my house. I'm going to try to find out if Leon got away with the gold before the law arrived."

Clay agreed and worked furiously following the man's plan. He could see that they dared not take the time to bury the outlaws, that this was the best he and his father could do for them. There were no lawmen, so the law must have taken any of their own wounded or dead back with them.

Clayton studied all the corpses, hoping not to find Orville

or Ty Rome. He was relieved when he didn't. Soon the body hauling was done. Clay went to the west end of the street and set fire to the first building on each side. He mounted the gray and, leading the copper dun, went up to the house on the hill.

On the way, Clay wondered if anyone had gotten away. Dammit, where were the Romes? he asked himself. Were Orville and Ty riding off somewhere even now, or had they been with the men who had surrendered and been taken into custody?

He dismounted at Merle's house. The killing had not been confined to the town below, for the gunman George lay dead on the porch with an empty six-gun in each hand. Clay stepped past him and opened the front door. The long hall looked the same as it had the other time he'd been there. He went down and opened the door to the room where he had first talked to the man.

Merle Hollister was there, bent over an opening in the floor. He whirled, with a gun in his hand. "Oh, Clay, it's you! I'll be ready to ride directly. We'll go out the back way. By the tracks I'd say that Leon got up the pack train I'd ordered and left several hours before the law got here. The lawmen didn't follow, but there are tracks from four horses that *did* go out in that direction. Most likely they were the only ones who got away."

He went back to what he'd been doing, and Clay realized he was loading pouches of money into saddlebags. Then Merle said, "Bring the horses to the back door, and I'll meet you there right away."

In only minutes he and Clay were riding up into the mountains. They traveled all day through country Clayton had never seen before. It got rougher and rougher. That night they camped at a fork in the trail. The tracks they'd been following had split. The pack train had gone more south, and the other four tracks, those whom Merle and Clay thought belonged to men who had gotten away after the raid, went west.

The man must have felt safe, because he stopped to camp overnight. Next morning he built a fire, and they had a meager meal with coffee.

Hollister said, "Come with me, Clay. We can catch Leon before he reaches Denver. We'll have all that gold, and, who knows? We might get along and stay together."

Clay didn't have to think long to form an answer. "I'd be lying if I said I'm not tempted and don't want to give it any thought. But I think I'll go the other way. Three of the tracks going west through the mountains look like the mounts and packhorse that the Romes were using."

He sipped some coffee before he continued. "I know my standards are different from yours. Or, for that matter, those most people think are right. But they're mine, and I'll go with them."

"Explain that to me," the man invited.

Clay finished his coffee and said, "The gold you're following and the money in your saddlebags has blood on it. But I earned the bank draft I got from the Romes through you by work I did for Orville and Ty. It doesn't matter how *they* got it."

Hollister looked into his steaming drink for a full minute. Then he raised his head. "I can't argue your right to have and to follow your own standards. That's what I always did. I know it must seem to you that mine changed when I came west, but they really didn't, Clay. It's just a different field of endeavor. I let other men do this kind of thing, and because I'm willing to take risks along with them, I demand my percentage off the top."

"But at The Settlement," Clay put in, "you directed jobs that took what you wanted from other people, and it didn't matter to you if the ones who got killed were innocent."

"There have always been different levels of people: those who never get off the bottom, those who get partway, and a rare few like you and me. We'd be at the top wherever we were."

Merle smiled at him, and Clay thought his father was proud of him. It was a new experience, because no one had ever shown pride in him before. He felt swayed and didn't like it that the man could be so convincing. Clay stood a moment with his head down, wondering what to do and how to answer. Then the thought of the McKennas and Hank came to him, and he stood taller.

"If I'm destined to be on top wherever I am, I'll make it at honest ranching in the New Mexico territory. I want to follow these other tracks, because I know without a doubt that the big one was made by that huge geld Ty Rome always rode. If the brothers are both alive, they'll be together. There has got to be some way for them to clear me without our getting arrested."

Clayton looked at Merle and smiled. A question lodged in that smile, a plea for understanding. He reached out a hand. "Shake on it, Father."

Hollister struggled with his disappointment, then stuck out his hand. "Take care of yourself, Clay."

They mounted and rode out. The man went south and his son, west.

About the Author

A.J. Arnold is the combined name of a married couple who work as a writing team. Their first Western novel, DEAD MAN'S CACHE, was published in 1988 by Ballantine Books.

The Arnolds are members of Western Writers of America (WWA).